D1559858

The Cowboy's Cover Girl

Lassoed Hearts Series, Volume 1

Janalyn Knight

Published by Janalyn Knight, 2021.

Chapter One

Knox McKinnis removed the halter from his big bay gelding and swatted him on the rump. The horse trotted off into the wheat pasture, seemingly unaffected by the long day sorting cattle on the 11,200-acre McKinnis ranch near the tiny town of Rule in north Texas. So close to west Texas that it shared the wild, desert landscape, the McKinnis property had its share of mesquite trees and prickly pear cactus. But the hardy natural grasses grew healthy white-tailed deer for the hunters that the ranch hosted each year and robust Black Angus cattle that were his father's pride.

After returning the halter to the big metal barn, he paused before entering the ranch house. Jessica's SUV was parked out front, which meant that his sister was back from the airport in Abilene. Should he head into Haskell for dinner? Meeting some stranger from New York wasn't high on his list after a hard day in the saddle. But what he really wanted was a shower and to hit the sack early. Better go in and get it over with.

As soon as he entered the big kitchen where everyone was already seated at the table, he locked eyes with Jessica's friend. He steeled himself to show no reaction at her revealing outfit, a lime-green satin jacket over a black crocheted top with holes easily two inches wide. Her tiny beige bra showed clearly underneath it. Was that what passed for acceptable fashion in

New York? He slid his glance away and headed to the sink to wash his hands.

When he took his seat at the table, Jessica spoke up. "Hey, brother, I'd like you to meet my friend, Sadie Stewart. Sadie, this is my big brother, Knox."

He nodded. "Pleased to meet you, ma'am."

Sadie raised her eyebrows. "I'm only twenty-six. Am I a ma'am already?"

He helped himself to a steak, biting back a smile. "In Texas, all women are ma'am."

"Well, isn't that nice."

He took a serving from the rest of the dishes without comment. He had nothing in common with the Northerner. Couldn't even imagine what would make a woman dress as she was. He took a bite of his fried potatoes and noticed that she only had a plate of salad in front of her. Didn't New Yorkers eat country food? He glanced up and noticed Jessica watching him.

"Sadie's a vegetarian."

He stifled a groan. Of course she was. He nodded and took a bite of green beans.

"Don't they have good Black Angus steaks in New York, Sadie?" his dad asked.

Sadie smiled. "I'm sure they do, Jeb. I just don't eat them."

"No wonder you're so skinny. A person could get sickly going without good beef," his father replied with a smile.

She obviously didn't take his comment personally because she returned his dad's smile. "I get plenty of protein, Jeb, I just don't eat animals in the process."

Knox took a quick bite of potatoes to keep from rolling his eyes. Did the city slicker have any idea how strange she sounded?

Maddie, Knox's mom, and always the peacemaker in the house, spoke up. "To each his own, I say. Sadie, I have to get groceries in Abilene this week. Why don't you come with me and we'll make sure you have plenty of meal choices from now on, okay?"

"That sounds wonderful, Maddie. Thank you."

She looked genuinely appreciative, and this appeased Knox some. But still. A vegetarian? Come on.

"So, how was your flight, Sadie?" his mother asked.

"It was fine. I guess I do so much of it that I don't pay much attention to flying anymore. The only thing that got my pulse racing was a tight time frame for my plane switch in Dallas. The little commuter I took to Abilene wasn't crowded, though, so that was nice."

"Well, we're sure glad you got here safely," his mom replied.

"It's great to be here, Maddie. Thanks so much for having me. This is a beautiful place. I've heard so much about Texas, and I can't wait to see a real working cattle ranch."

He pressed his lips together. *Damn.* That didn't sound good. Did Jessica have plans for the two of them to follow him around?

"Sadie and I'll do the cleanup after dinner, Mom," Jessica offered.

Sadie's head bobbed up, and her eyes widened in surprise.

His lips tightened. What? Didn't she ever do dishes where she came from?

"Um, do you have gloves?" Sadie asked.

"I don't think so, but we can get some. You can dry tonight," his sister answered.

Sadie smiled. "That sounds perfect."

Well, she'd taken that in stride. Maybe there was more to the woman than met the eyes. He finished the last of his food and went to the sink to rinse off his plate.

"It was nice meeting you, Knox."

He put his plate in the dishwasher before replying. "Welcome to the McKinnis Ranch, Miss Stewart."

"Oh, call me Sadie, please."

He nodded. "Good evening, Sadie." He strode from the room, wondering just how long the strange woman from New York City would be staying.

SADIE FINISHED DRYING the plate and stacked it in the overhead cabinet with the others. There was surprising comfort in this everyday task. At her condo in the city, she had a housekeeper who took care of chores like this. She also dropped off and picked up her dry-cleaning, and handled a variety of other chores that made Sadie's life easier. With her annual modeling salary in the millions, there wasn't much in life that Sadie couldn't pay for, and skimping on staff and necessities was something she never did.

As one of the world's top supermodels, her life was incredibly fast-paced. It took everything from her. She'd become jaded with the world, burnt out with the fashion industry, with the backstabbing and hateful gossip, and with the constant travel and being on display every moment. That was the reason she'd sought refuge here with Jessica on her isolated Texas ranch.

In the past months, life had lost its meaning, food its appeal. When she'd fainted in the middle of a shoot, she'd realized that she'd reached her breaking point. She'd called Jessica and asked if she could come to Texas.

And what an unlikely pair they were. They'd met while Jessica was studying art at NYU and working in a coffee shop. Sadie had come in, stressed and out of sorts. Jessica's sunny disposition and natural kindness had breached Sadie's black mood and, over the next few weeks, they'd become friends.

She and Jessica had stayed in touch after she'd moved back to Texas and become a teacher, FaceTiming and texting several times a week. Sadie had come to lean on her pragmatic, down-to-earth friend for advice and a sane voice in the chaos of her world-traveling life.

Jessica handed Sadie the last bowl. "How about we go outside? I'll show you around the place."

"I'd like that."

As they walked through the living room, Maddie looked up from the quilt square that she was working on. "Thanks for cleaning up, girls."

Jessica and Sadie replied in unison, "You're welcome."

A few moments later, they stood at the pasture fence, where a small herd of horses grazed. Jessica pointed to a sorrel mare. "That one there, the one that's kind of orangey red? She's mine."

"She's beautiful. What breed is she?"

"We have Quarter Horses here on the ranch. They're the most suited to working with cattle. Would you like me to catch her up? We could brush her. She loves that."

"Oh, that would be wonderful!" Sadie looked down at her heels. "I'm not really dressed for this, am I?"

Jessica grinned. "Not at all. Do you want to change first?"

That would take time. Did it really matter? She didn't have much in the way of ranch clothes in her wardrobe, and she'd been so exhausted before she came that she hadn't been able to face going shopping. "No, I'm fine like this."

"Just don't get stepped on with those pretty pink-painted toenails sticking out of your shoes."

Soon, the mare was tied in the barn, and Jessica handed Sadie a brush. "Look at the way the hair grows and brush in that direction. She'll love it."

Sadie examined the mare's back and made her first stroke as Jessica moved to the horse's other side to work. Soon, she had a rhythm going with her strokes and the mare's head lowered. She was obviously loving the attention. Sadie stopped and moved to her beautiful head, petting the round, muscular cheek and looking into the mare's large brown eyes. Her calm gaze soothed Sadie's soul. She kissed the horse's muzzle, smelling the fresh grass on her breath. Sadie closed her eyes and inhaled again. This is what life should be about.

Footsteps sounded at the barn entrance and she opened her eyes. Knox strode into the barn, a rifle on his arm, his gaze taking in the sight of her holding the horse's head. He glanced away and moved to the shelves on the wall.

"What's up, brother?" Jessica asked.

"Got to dart a bull in the morning."

"Really? What's going on?

Sadie listened attentively, her eyes never leaving his hands as he pulled medicine from the fridge and loaded a dart.

"Vet's coming in the morning. Bull's got an abscess. He's hell to load without tranking him." He capped the dart and stuck it in his shirt pocket.

She couldn't take her eyes from him. His economical movements spoke of long practice. He was so self-assured.

Jessica headed for the tack room. A few seconds later, she called out, "I can't find a hoof pick."

Knox let out a long sigh and headed that way.

Sadie grinned. That was so like a big brother.

Jessica came out brandishing the pick. "Can't bring a horse in without cleaning its hooves."

Knox returned to the workbench and the rifle.

Sadie stared at him. What made this man tick? Why was he so reticent? Men usually stared at her. Wanted to talk to her. He wouldn't even look at her. It felt odd. He didn't seem like the shy type. He just appeared uninterested, and for some reason that bothered her.

Jessica looked up, "Have you ridden before, Sadie?"

She smiled lopsidedly. "I don't know if you'd call it riding. I had a perfume photoshoot where I had to climb on a huge Saddlebred horse. He was beautiful, but he was really nervous with everything going on around us. All I knew about riding was what the owner told me right before he boosted me up into the little saddle. The guy showed me how to hold the reins, and then I was on my own. The poor horse kept shying off every time the camera clicked. I was supposed to look accomplished and carefree in my spiffy riding outfit."

"Oh Lord. How did you keep from falling off?" Jessica asked.

Sadie glanced at Knox. She could tell that he was following the conversation. "I wasn't about to fall off. It was an important shoot. I just pretended to be someone else, someone who knew how to ride, and I got through the afternoon just fine."

Jessica raised her brows. "That's a neat trick."

Sadie smiled. "I have to use it from time to time when photographers spring crazy things on me."

As Jessica cleaned the mare's hooves, she asked, "Can we go with you tomorrow, Knox? I'm sure Sadie would love to watch you work cattle."

His glance slid to Sadie, then away. Putting the vial of tranquilizer back into the fridge, he kept silent. Finally, on his way out of the barn, he said, "Suit yourselves."

Jessica rolled her eyes and grinned at Sadie. "A man of few words, my brother."

Sadie sighed. "I don't think he likes me."

"Don't worry about it. He's a pretty serious guy. I'm sure most people find him pretty hard to get to know." She untied the mare. "Let's turn her out and get back to the house."

Sadie's gaze slid outside to where Knox stood at his truck. The handsome cowboy was an enigma. She inspected his fine-looking butt. And a man she might want to get to know.

Chapter Two

Knox McKinnis removed the halter from his big bay gelding and swatted him on the rump. The horse trotted off into the wheat pasture, seemingly unaffected by the long day sorting cattle on the 11,200-acre McKinnis ranch near the tiny town of Rule in north Texas. So close to west Texas that it shared the wild, desert landscape, the McKinnis property had its share of mesquite trees and prickly pear cactus. But the hardy natural grasses grew healthy white-tailed deer for the hunters that the ranch hosted each year and robust Black Angus cattle that were his father's pride.

After returning the halter to the big metal barn, he paused before entering the ranch house. Jessica's SUV was parked out front, which meant that his sister was back from the airport in Abilene. Should he head into Haskell for dinner? Meeting some stranger from New York wasn't high on his list after a hard day in the saddle.

But what he really wanted was a shower and to hit the sack early. Better go in and get it over with.

As soon as he entered the big kitchen where everyone was already seated at the table, he locked eyes with Jessica's friend. He steeled himself to show no reaction to her revealing outfit, a lime-green satin jacket over a black crocheted top with holes easily two inches wide. Her tiny beige bra showed clearly underneath it. Was that what passed for acceptable fashion in New York? He slid his glance away and headed to the sink to wash his hands.

When he took his seat at the table, Jessica spoke up. "Hey, brother, I'd like you to meet my friend, Sadie Stewart. Sadie, this is my big brother, Knox."

He nodded. "Pleased to meet you, ma'am."

Sadie raised her eyebrows. "I'm only twenty-six. Am I a ma'am already?"

He helped himself to a steak, biting back a smile. "In Texas, all women are ma'am."

"Well, isn't that nice."

He took a serving from the rest of the dishes without comment. He had nothing in common with the Northerner. Couldn't even imagine what would make a woman dress as she was. He took a bite of his fried potatoes and noticed that she only had a plate of salad in front of her. Didn't New Yorkers eat country food? He glanced up and noticed Jessica watching him.

"Sadie's a vegetarian."

He stifled a groan. Of course she was. He nodded and took a bite of green beans.

"Don't they have good Black Angus steaks in New York, Sadie?" his dad asked.

Sadie smiled. "I'm sure they do, Jeb. I just don't eat them."

"No wonder you're so skinny. A person could get sickly going without good beef," his father replied with a smile.

She obviously didn't take his comment personally because she returned his dad's smile. "I get plenty of protein, Jeb, I just don't eat animals in the process."

Knox took a quick bite of potatoes to keep from rolling his eyes. Did the city slicker have any idea how strange she sounded?

Maddie, Knox's mom, and always the peacemaker in the house, spoke up. "To each his own, I say. Sadie, I have to get groceries in Abilene this week. Why don't you come with me and we'll make sure you have plenty of meal choices from now on, okay?"

"That sounds wonderful, Maddie. Thank you."

She looked genuinely appreciative, and this appeased Knox some. But still. A vegetarian? Come on.

"So, how was your flight, Sadie?" his mother asked.

"It was fine. I guess I do so much of it that I don't pay much attention to flying anymore. The only thing that got my pulse racing was a tight time frame for my plane switch in Dallas. The little commuter I took to Abilene wasn't crowded, though, so that was nice."

"Well, we're sure glad you got here safely," his mom replied.

"It's great to be here, Maddie. Thanks so much for having me. This is a beautiful place. I've heard so much about Texas, and I can't wait to see a real working cattle ranch."

He pressed his lips together. *Damn.* That didn't sound good. Did Jessica have plans for the two of them to follow him around?

"Sadie and I'll do the cleanup after dinner, Mom," Jessica offered.

Sadie's head bobbed up, and her eyes widened in surprise.

What? Didn't she ever do dishes where she came from?

"Um, do you have gloves?" Sadie asked.

"I don't think so, but we can get some. You can dry tonight," his sister answered.

Sadie smiled. "That sounds perfect."

Well, she'd taken that in stride. Maybe there was more to the woman than met the eyes. He finished the last of his food and went to the sink to rinse off his plate.

"It was nice meeting you, Knox."

He put his plate in the dishwasher before replying. "Welcome to the McKinnis Ranch, Miss Stewart."

"Oh, call me Sadie, please."

He nodded. "Good evening, Sadie." He strode from the room, wondering just how long the strange woman from New York City would be staying.

SADIE FINISHED DRYING the plate and stacked it in the overhead cabinet with the others. There was surprising comfort in this everyday but unfamiliar task. At her condo in the city, she had a housekeeper who took care of chores like this. The housekeeper also dropped off and picked up the dry-cleaning, and handled a variety of other chores that made Sadie's life easier. With Sadie's annual modeling salary in the millions, there wasn't much in life that she couldn't pay for, and skimping on staff and necessities was something she never did.

As one of the world's top supermodels, her life was incredibly fast-paced. The travel, the adoration of her fans, it all had been wonderful at first.

But in the end it took everything from her. She'd become jaded with the world, burnt out with the fashion industry, with the backstabbing and hateful gossip, and with the constant travel and being on display every moment. That was the reason she'd sought refuge here with Jessica on her isolated Texas ranch.

In the past months, life had lost its meaning, food its appeal. When she'd fainted in the middle of a shoot, she'd realized that she'd reached her breaking point. She'd called Jessica and asked if she could come to Texas.

And what an unlikely pair they were. They'd met while Jessica was studying art at NYU and working in a coffee shop. Sadie had come in, stressed and out of sorts from a long, demanding shoot. Jessica's sunny disposition and natural kindness had breached Sadie's black mood and, over the next few weeks, they'd become friends.

She and Jessica had stayed in touch after she'd moved back to Texas and become a teacher, FaceTiming and texting several times a week. Sadie had come to lean on her pragmatic, down-to-earth friend for advice and a sane voice in the chaos of her world-traveling life.

Jessica handed Sadie the last bowl. "How about we go outside? I'll show you around the place."

"I'd like that."

As they walked through the living room, Maddie looked up from the quilt square that she was working on. "Thanks for cleaning up, girls."

Jessica and Sadie replied in unison, "You're welcome."

A few moments later, they stood at the pasture fence, where a small herd of horses grazed. Jessica pointed to a sorrel mare. "That one there, the one that's kind of orangey red? She's mine."

"She's beautiful. What breed is she?"

"We have Quarter Horses here on the ranch. They're the most suited to working with cattle. Would you like me to catch her up? We could brush her. She loves that."

"Oh, that would be wonderful!" Sadie looked down at her heels. "I'm not really dressed for this, am I?"

Jessica grinned. "Not at all. Do you want to change first?"

That would take time. Did it really matter? She didn't have much in the way of ranch clothes in her wardrobe, and she'd been so exhausted before she came that she hadn't been able to face going shopping. "No, I'm fine like this."

"Just don't get stepped on with those pretty pink-painted toenails sticking out of your shoes."

Soon, the mare was tied in the barn, and Jessica handed Sadie a brush. "Look at the way the hair grows and brush in that direction. She'll love it."

Sadie examined the mare's back and made her first stroke as Jessica moved to the horse's other side to work. Soon, she had a rhythm going with her strokes. The mare's head lowered. She was obviously loving the attention. Sadie stopped and moved to her beautiful head, petting the round, muscular cheek and looking into the mare's large brown eyes. Her calm gaze soothed Sadie's soul. She kissed the horse's muzzle, smelling the fresh grass on her breath. Sadie closed her eyes and inhaled again. This is what life should be about.

Footsteps sounded at the barn entrance and she opened her eyes. Knox strode into the barn, a rifle on his arm, his gaze taking in the sight of Sadie holding the horse's head. He glanced away and moved to the shelves on the wall.

"What's up, brother?" Jessica asked.

"Got to dart a bull tomorrow."

"Really? What's going on?

Sadie listened attentively, her eyes never leaving his hands as he pulled medicine from the fridge and loaded a dart.

"Vet's coming in the morning. Bull's got an abscess. He's hell to load without tranking him." He capped the dart and stuck it in his shirt pocket.

She couldn't take her eyes from him. His economical movements spoke of long practice. He was so self-assured.

Jessica headed for the tack room. A few seconds later, she called out, "I can't find a hoof pick."

Knox let out a long sigh and headed that way.

Sadie grinned. That was so like a big brother.

Jessica came out brandishing the pick. "Can't bring a horse in without cleaning its hooves."

Knox returned to the workbench and the rifle.

Sadie stared at him. What made this man tick? Why was he so reticent? Men usually stared at her. Wanted to talk to her. He wouldn't even look at her. It felt odd. He didn't seem like the shy type. He just appeared uninterested, and for some reason that bothered her.

Jessica looked up, "Have you ridden before, Sadie?"

She smiled lopsidedly. "I don't know if you'd call it riding. I had a perfume photoshoot where I had to climb on a huge Saddlebred horse. He was beautiful, but he was really nervous with everything going on around us. All I knew about riding was what the owner told me right before he boosted me up into the little saddle. The guy showed me how to hold the reins, and then I was on my own. The poor horse kept shying off every time the camera clicked. I was supposed to look accomplished and carefree in my spiffy riding outfit."

"Oh Lord. How did you keep from falling off?" Jessica asked.

Sadie glanced at Knox. She could tell that he was following the conversation. "I wasn't about to fall off. It was an important shoot. All I really needed was confidence. So I just pretended to be someone else, someone who knew how to ride, and I got through the afternoon just fine."

Jessica raised her brows. "That's a neat trick."

Sadie smiled. "I have to use it from time to time when photographers spring crazy things on me."

As Jessica cleaned the mare's hooves, she asked, "Can we go with you tomorrow, Knox? I'm sure Sadie would love to watch you work cattle."

His glance slid to Sadie, then away. Putting the vial of tranquilizer back into the fridge, he kept silent. Finally, on his way out of the barn, he said, "Suit yourselves."

Jessica rolled her eyes and grinned at Sadie. "A man of few words, my brother."

Sadie sighed. "I don't think he likes me."

"Don't worry about it. He's a pretty serious guy. I'm sure most people find him pretty hard to get to know." She untied the mare. "Let's turn her out and get back to the house."

Sadie's gaze slid outside to where Knox stood at his truck. The handsome cowboy was an enigma. She inspected his fine-looking butt. And a man she might want to get to know.

Chapter Two

Knox stepped out of the truck in the south pasture, refusing to glance over at his sister's SUV, where she and her New York guest sat in the open back watching every move he made. Why he felt nervous was a mystery to him. Everything he was about to do was old hat as far as ranch work went. He strode to the back of the trailer and opened the gate, then climbed inside and latched the middle gate open too.

He'd parked near the herd of Black Angus cattle where the bull, nicknamed The Beast because he had such an ornery disposition, had his head up and was watching every move Knox made. He'd told the girls to stay in their vehicle. There was no telling what that ornery bastard would get into his head to do if he got riled up.

Knox unloaded his big bay gelding and mounted. The dogs had ridden with him in the truck, and they trotted over awaiting instructions. First, he needed to dart the already nervous bull. Edging his horse nearer the herd, he raised the rifle and got a bead on the bull's massive hip, then pulled the trigger.

The dart hit the bull square on the hip. The bull jerked and snorted, trotting through the herd, knocking cows out of his way as he went. Knox whistled for the dogs and followed the bull as he exited the herd, commanding the dogs "Away to me," which told them to move counterclockwise to head the bull toward the trailer. He didn't care if the bull made it over there or not at this point. The big animal was agitated and needed time for the sedative to work. Knox just didn't want him running off in the meantime.

He glanced at the SUV and found Sadie's eyes glued to him. A tickle of excitement raced up his nerves, and he scowled. What the hell was that about? Then the bull trotted off a little way and turned and faced the herd. Knox called out, "Down." The dogs instantly lay on their bellies. He sat his horse and waited as the medicine worked its way into the bull's body. They were at a standoff.

A few minutes later, the bull's head lowered. Knox moved forward and called, "Away to me." The dogs were instantly up and after the bull. Using verbal commands, he guided the dogs as they slowly herded the bull to the trailer with nips to his heels. The bull, seeing the open gate, suddenly turned away. Knox called, "Come by. Come by." The dogs immediately moved clockwise, snapping at the bull's heels and hocks and turning him back to the trailer. Knox rode in close as the dogs urged the bull up and into the trailer. He quickly dismounted and shut the middle door.

Jessica called, "Way to go, brother!"

He glanced over and saw that Sadie had a wide grin on her face. Again, a little thrill raced along his nerves. He loaded the gelding into the back of the trailer. When he got back to the truck, he looked at Jessica and twirled his index finger in the air.

She nodded and started her SUV.

Back at the ranch, he unloaded his horse and tied him in the barn, then backed the trailer up to the pen with the hydraulic squeeze chute and unloaded the bull. The women came into the barn and watched as he unsaddled the gelding.

"That bull is huge," Sadie said.

"Nearly two thousand pounds." He lifted and then tugged the saddle off the horse's tall withers.

"Oh my God. That big? He looked kind of mean when he ran out of the trailer."

Knox glanced at her before he headed to the tack room. "He is mean. Most of my bulls are easy to handle. Angus cattle are pretty docile for the most part. I call this one The Beast for good reason."

"The Beast?" she repeated. "Man, that sounds scary."

He walked back from the tack room and nodded. "I keep an eye on him when I'm on foot. There've been times when he'd have loved to get a piece of me."

With quick strokes of his arm, he brushed the gelding down. Having Sadie's gaze on him was actually making him a little nervous, and that was just plain damn crazy. He tossed the brush into a nearby bucket and untied his horse, glad he could leave the barn and the beautiful woman behind while he turned the gelding out to pasture.

Knox strode from the barn, his gelding following close behind him.

"How old is your horse?"

What? Had she followed him? Those crazy shoes of hers, totally inappropriate for being out on a ranch, sure were quiet on the grass. He didn't look at her. "Bronco's seven."

"Why's he called Bronco?"

He gritted his teeth. "He was a tough one to break."

"Oh, so you trained him yourself?"

He stopped and turned around to look at her, fixing her with a stare, hoping she'd go away. "I train all our horses."

"Oh," she said quietly. When he continued on, she didn't follow.

Good. The last thing he needed was a city-girl shadow.

As he closed the pasture gate, a movement in the driveway caught his attention. The vet had just pulled up in his truck loaded with medical supplies. Knox lengthened his stride and met the vet as he stepped out his door. "Thanks for coming, Steve."

They shook hands. "No problem, Knox. So, you've got a bull with an abscess?"

"Yeah, it's a big one."

Steve gave a wry grin. "The bull or the abscess?"

"Both."

"Okay, let me get my stuff, and I'll meet you in the corral."

Knox whistled up the dogs and hurried to the pen. They scooted under the lowest bar and danced around, excited to work. He opened the gate to the alley leading to the chute and commanded the dogs, "Come around!"

As the dogs approached, the bull lowered his head, like he might be looking for a fight. The sedative was obviously starting to wear off. One dog got behind him and nipped his heels. The other moved to the side to prevent the bull from going in the wrong direction. Then the bull caved and headed docilely for the alley, obviously still too sedated to put up much of a fight. The dogs kept on his heels until he entered the chute and Knox locked him in the head gate.

Jessica and Sadie walked up.

Knox turned to them. "You two can watch, but stay out of the way."

"What's wrong with him?" Sadie asked.

He motioned to the bull's beefy hind leg. "He's got a big abscess. The doc's going to treat it." Then he took pity on her. "Go ahead. Have a look. Just don't stick your hand in there. You could get your arm broken."

He approached with her, not quite trusting her to follow directions. But she stood clear, looking closely.

"Is it that big swelling above his knee? That's huge."

"Yes, and that knee is called a hock on cattle."

She glanced at him. "Oh." The bull snorted loudly, and she startled. "He's so big. Gigantic even. I never realized cattle were so large."

The vet approached, and she stepped back, meeting Knox's gaze. "Thanks for letting me look."

She had gorgeous dark-chocolate-colored eyes, and they did something to him. Unsettled, he turned to Steve. "Got everything you need?"

"Think so." The man glanced at the women. "I've got an audience today."

Jessica smiled. "Steve, this is my friend from New York, Sadie Stewart. Sadie, this is our long-time vet, Steve Jensen."

Sadie put out her hand. "Pleased to meet you, Dr. Jensen."

Steve smiled and shook her hand. "The pleasure's mine, Sadie, and please, call me Steve." He set his supplies down on an old wooden spool discarded by the telephone company on some long-ago day and rescued by Knox's father for just that purpose. Next, he peered through the bars of the chute and examined the bull. "That's going to make a mess."

Knox glanced at Sadie, but she didn't look like she understood what was coming. Would she throw up? How strong was her stomach?

Steve picked up a scalpel blade and reached through the bars, making a quick, two-inch incision in the huge abscess. The bull *maawed* and launched himself at the head gate, but he couldn't get away. A thick pink stream of pus squirted out from the tightly swollen mound and then poured down the bull's leg. When the flow started to ebb, Steve pressed on the sides of the abscess, and chunky blobs of infection poured out of the opening.

Knox looked at Sadie, surprised to see an avid look of interest on her face instead of revulsion.

As the vet worked, Sadie asked surprisingly intelligent questions. He'd obviously underestimated the Easterner. After flushing the abscess with hydrogen peroxide and giving the animal a shot of antibiotics, Steve slapped the bull on his haunches. "All done. I'll send you a bill, Knox. Nice seeing you. And Sadie? Glad you didn't faint." He grinned as he walked off.

"Never happen," Sadie called after him and laughed.

As Knox prepared to load the bull back into the trailer, he could feel Sadie's intent gaze on him, watching his every move. He admired the way she'd held up through the gory procedure on the bull. He hadn't expected that. She actually appeared to have enjoyed the whole thing. The dogs ran the bull through the loading chute and up into the trailer.

Sadie called out, "You're really good at this."

He looked back at her. "I should be. Been doing it all my life." Despite himself, though, her words made him feel good.

He reached through the bars as the bull spun to face the back of the trailer and slammed the middle gate shut.

While he pulled the truck forward, he realized that he'd come to admire the New Yorker, maybe just a little. He got out to shut the back trailer gate and glanced over his shoulder. He couldn't help himself. She was still there, watching, although Jessica had already left for the house.

As he drove off, he looked in his rearview mirror. Sadie raised her arm and waved goodbye. His heart lurched. He stuck his arm out the window and waved back, a prick of interest in the beautiful woman sneaking up on him. Today had proved something. There was more to the city-slicker friend of his sister's than he'd originally given her credit for. And he was glad.

SADIE TIED HER HIGH-topped, old-school-style sneakers and stood up in the one pair of jeans that she'd hurriedly packed before catching her plane. The faded denim fit her body perfectly, and her T-shirt, casual yet just the right size to display her figure, with a French tuck at her small waist.

Jessica poked her head in at the door. "Ready?"

Sadie tucked a lip gloss in her pocket. "I sure am."

Her friend grinned. "Come on. We'll watch the guys rope from under a big oak tree. It'll be cool in the shade." Before leaving the house, she grabbed two folding lawn chairs from the back porch and a small cooler from the kitchen. She gestured to two wine glasses. "Carry those, please. We're watching in style tonight."

Sadie smiled. "Let me carry the cooler, too, silly. You've got the chairs."

As they were getting set up under the oak tree, Knox arrived with a trailer load of Black Angus calves. Jessica went over to open the arena gate for him as he backed up to it. The trailer came to a stop and, as she opened its gate, the calves came jumping out. They trotted around the arena, the livelier ones bucking a time or two. Jessica shut the trailer, and Knox pulled away.

"That's a lot of calves," Sadie said.

"Yeah, there'll be four cowboys roping tonight," Jessica said.

Sadie leaned on the pipe gate and peered through the bars. The calves had settled down now and were mostly just staring at their surroundings.

Knox rode up to the arena gate on his big bay gelding, a rope tied to the front of his saddle.

"Those calves are so big. I was expecting little babies," Sadie said as Jessica opened the gate for her brother.

He glanced at Sadie. "Rodeo rules state that roping calves must be a minimum of 250 pounds. These calves are about 250 to 280 pounds. Once they get much bigger, we don't rope them anymore."

"Oh."

He whistled at the dogs and called, "Away to me." The dogs began rounding up the calves. With their expert help, the calves were soon moved into the holding pen at the end of the arena.

Sadie glanced over her shoulder as a truck pulling a two-horse trailer drove into the ranch drive.

Jessica waved. "That's Blake Haggerty and his little brother, Jason. Jason runs the chute for the ropers." She turned back to

Sadie. "All of the guys donate calves for the Friday night prac-
tices. Once they get too big to rope, the guys take them home
and bring some more. That way Knox doesn't have to come up
with a whole herd of roping calves."

Blake pulled to the far side of the arena and stopped. A moment later he unloaded a tall sorrel gelding from the trailer.

Sadie watched as he slipped a bridle over the horse's halter,
then mounted and headed for the arena gate. A younger guy
pulled a medium-sized ice chest from the back seat of the truck
and followed after him. To her surprise, instead of dismounting
to open the gate, Blake leaned down from the saddle and
opened it. His horse moved sideways, then slipped around it
and into the arena as Blake shut the gate again. She looked at
Jessica and grinned. "That was amazing."

"What? The gate thing?"

"Yeah. That horse is smart."

Jessica smiled. "Cowboys have lots of tricks like that to save
them work." She poured each of them a glass of wine, and they
sipped the cool beverage as the other two cowboys arrived and
unloaded their horses. Then Jessica stood up. "Come on. Let's
go where the action is." She led Sadie to the fence near the roping boxes and the chute.

Knox whistled up the dogs and they came running over. He
started toward the back pen on his horse and pointed. "Bring
'em up!" This was something the dogs obviously knew from
experience. They raced to the holding pen and nipped and
barked, heading the calves up the alley and toward the front of
the arena. Knox waited. When they were all in the holding pen,
he closed the alley gate.

Jason ran some of them into the narrow alley leading to the chute and put a pipe behind the last one so he couldn't back out. Then he opened the head gate slightly and caught the lead calf's head firmly. He was ready for the first roper. The loose calves milled around the small holding pen, watching what was going on around them.

Knox rode over, and Sadie asked, "How many calves are you roping tonight?"

"Twenty."

"That's all? That won't take long, with four of you."

"We run them all through several times."

She nodded, embarrassed that she hadn't thought of this.

Now all of the cowboys were in the arena and warming up their horses, loping around at the fence line, making their loops and swinging them alongside their mounts.

Jessica pointed. "That's what they call 'shaking out the kinks.'"

Sadie and Jessica returned to their lawn chairs and a few seconds later, Knox rode by. His gaze met Sadie's for a brief instant, and tingles raced through her. His usual guarded look had been replaced with one of interest. Could it be that he didn't dislike her after all? His slim, sexy hips swayed in the saddle to his big gelding's easy lope. It had been a long time since she'd been attracted to a man. Why did it have to be this taciturn cowboy?

She examined each man closely as he rode by. Were all Texas cowboys hunks, or were these guys just the picks of the litter? Tall, broad-shouldered, and with just the right amount of muscle, they must have women after them wherever they went.

The horse Ryder rode was really beautiful. Jessica called it a dapple-gray gelding. It had blueish smudgy spots all over its pale gray body and was a striking specimen of horseflesh.

Knox pulled up to a halt at the roping boxes, and the others followed. They spoke quietly for a moment, then Blake entered the right-hand box and backed his horse into the corner. Jason's eyes were glued to him, awaiting his signal. Blake's horse's ears pointed toward the chute, his full attention on the calf. The cowboy nodded, and Jason yanked on the lever.

The head gate shot open, and the calf flew out of the chute, breaking into top speed. Blake's horse was after him in a flash. Blake threw his loop. It looked like his rope was already tied to the saddle horn. As soon as the loop left his hand, Blake swung from the saddle, his hand following his rope to the calf, which had just been yanked to a stop.

He grabbed the calf's flank and front leg, and with a kick from his knee, brought it to the ground on its side. Holding it down with the weight of his knee, he tied the back legs and one front leg together with a smaller rope and threw his hands in the air, the signal for the time to stop.

Sadie gave Jessica a worried look. "That looks so rough."

Jessica nodded. "It seems like it, but the calves are fine. Just watch. That one'll get up and walk off like nothing ever happened."

And it did. That reassured Sadie, but it still seemed like an awful experience for the young animals. The calf trotted to the end of the arena and stood quietly.

Next up was Ryder, and he, too, caught his calf. But, after he'd tied it, the animal gave a mighty struggle and one leg came loose. The other cowboys catcalled in a good-humored way, and Ryder grinned and shook his head.

"That right there would have ruined him in a rodeo," Jessica explained.

Sadie took a sip of wine. There was more to this calf roping than just a good throw.

When Knox entered the box, he gave a quick look in their direction. Was he worried about his performance because she was watching? That hardly seemed in character with the tough cowboy persona he wore.

The calf burst out of the gate with Knox right behind him. The cowboy caught him quickly and flew out of the saddle, running at top speed to flank and throw the calf. His hands blurred and then flew into the air.

Sadie caught her breath at the speed of it.

The calf struggled but stayed tied. One of the cowboys whistled loudly in admiration. The others called out in appreciation.

Jessica yelled, "Woohoo, brother!"

Sadie clapped loudly as Knox untied the calf and it got up and trotted off.

He glanced in her direction, and their gazes locked. Her hands stilled. He looked into her eyes—what was he searching for? The corner of his mouth tilted up, and her breath caught. She sucked in a breath and returned the smile.

Then he called out to the other guys, and the moment was over.

She raised her hand to her throat and looked at Jessica.

Her friend gave her a knowing smile. "You don't have to tell me. My brother's a hunk."

Sadie took a long drink of wine, then reached for the bottle. "Well, hell."

Jessica laughed.

After the last calf had been run through the chute, the guys took a break. The horses and the calves needed a breather. After tying their horses to the arena fence, they all retrieved beers from their ice chests and stood around to shoot the breeze.

"Come on. I'll introduce you around." Jessica stood and headed for the arena gate.

The cowboys watched their approach with interest, and all conversation stopped as Jessica opened the gate.

She approached the group and grinned. "You all can stop staring now. This is my good friend, Sadie Stewart. She's from New York City." She gestured to a tall, blond cowboy. "Sadie, this is Blake Haggerty."

He stepped forward and reached out his hand, shaking with a gentleness that surprised her. "Pleased to meet you, ma'am."

She smiled. "Please, everyone, call me Sadie."

Jessica nodded to the next cowboy. "Sadie, meet Ryder Booth." The handsome, dark-haired cowboy took a step forward and offered his hand. "Nice to meet you, Sadie."

"Thank you, Ryder."

A tall, broad-shouldered, black-headed young man stepped forward, a big grin on his face as he thrust his hand out. "Josh Rowder. Welcome to Texas, Sadie."

She smiled at his enthusiasm and shook his hand. "Why, thank you, Josh. I love it here, and I'm excited at everything I'm learning about ranching."

Josh flicked a glance at Knox. "Well, if you ever want a tour of my place, just have Jessica give me a holler. My ranch is about thirty minutes from here."

Knox threw his empty beer can into a metal barrel with a loud crash and said loudly, "Let's get back to it!"

The others hurriedly finished their beers and strode for their horses.

Sadie watched Knox as he stalked off toward his gelding. She'd wanted to ask him how The Beast was doing now that his wound had had a few days to heal. Was Knox angry because Josh had invited her to visit his ranch? If so, what did that mean? He didn't look her way as he whistled the dogs up and directed them to bring the calves to the front of the arena.

Over the next hour, however, as the men roped the next pen of calves, she looked over to find Knox staring at her more than once.

At the next breather, she and Jessica joined the guys again, and the cowboys chatted easily with her. All of them, that is, except Knox. He looked at her plenty, though.

"What's it like to be a fashion model?" Ryder asked.

She rolled her eyes. "A lot of hard work and more travel than anyone would ever choose to do."

"I'll bet it's fun, though," Josh said.

She shrugged. "In the beginning, although it was really hard work, I remember thinking it was fun." Memories of her terrible experience at fourteen came flooding back, and she bit her lip. "But there's a very dark side to modeling that most people don't know."

"That doesn't sound good," Blake said.

"It's not. I learned early that I needed to protect myself, and I figured out how. Now I work hard and stay away from the booze and drugs that take a lot of girls down."

"But don't you like getting to see all of those cool places?" he asked.

She grimaced. "I don't get to see all that much. I fly in and do my shoot and then I'm off to the next assignment. Sometimes there're parties that I have to be seen at, those kinds of things. But really, it's just frantically hard work."

She glanced at Knox. He had a grim look on his face. Did he dislike her talking to his friends like this?

"Well, if you wanted a change of pace, you came to the right place," Ryder said. "Life on a cattle ranch is busy, but not anything like that."

She smiled. "I'm loving my time here. And this is gorgeous country. I love how wild and unspoiled it is."

Blake grinned. "Nobody in their right mind would dislike Texas."

Everyone laughed.

Knox abruptly whistled to the dogs and called, "Bring 'em up!"

She caught him looking at her several times while the men were roping the last pen of calves, but she couldn't read his expression.

At the end of the night, each cowboy stopped to say goodbye before returning to their vehicles, a fact that didn't escape Knox's notice. His unforgiving mouth was pressed into a thin line. Was he jealous, she wondered? But how could he be? He didn't give her the time of day.

Knox backed up the trailer to the loading chute, and he and the dogs loaded the calves into the trailer. Then he pulled forward, and Jessica shut the trailer gate. He left without a backward glance.

Sadie stared as the trailer disappeared into the darkness. What the hell was going on with that handsome, cantankerous cowboy?

Chapter Three

Knox waited in the living room, thinking again that he was making a big mistake. Jessica had asked him to go out with her and her boyfriend, Scott, on a double date with Sadie, of all people. Footsteps sounded in the hallway, and Jessica walked in, looking pretty in a knee-length dress. Then his jaw dropped.

Sadie came right behind her in a floor-length white outfit that started with a satiny bra top. The attached dress crossed in front before draping to a slit hemline that revealed glimpses of her long legs. She was stunning. Her long, ebony hair curled below her shoulders, and he couldn't take his eyes off her.

His mouth snapped shut. She was wearing *that* to the movies?

Her gaze strayed to him, traveling up and down his body, as if appraising his normal get-up for going out—starched Wranglers, dress belt with one of his rodeo trophy buckles, starched dress shirt, and his best boots. Her eyes widened when he raised his black felt hat to his head. He clenched his teeth. *That's right, dammit! I'm going cowboy all the way tonight, Miss New York. Live with it.*

His mother answered a knock at the door.

His gaze never left Sadie.

Maddie said, "Come in, Scott. I think everyone's ready."

Knox turned away. He desperately regretted giving into his baby sister's plea. A hand encircled his arm, and he stiffened.

"You look nice tonight, Knox. I've never been on a date with a handsome cowboy before."

Was Sadie being a smartass, or had that been a serious comment? He glanced down at her. She had a sweet smile on her face. He relaxed a little. Maybe she'd meant it after all. He chewed the corner of his mouth. Was he crazy here? Had she really looked at him with disdain a minute ago? What was it about this Easterner that turned him inside out?

Out on the porch, he said, "I'm happy to drive tonight."

"I've got it," Scott said. "We invited you all, right?"

Knox swallowed a groan. He detested riding in the back seat. There was never enough room for his long legs, so he rode all scrunched up the entire time.

He opened the back door and helped Sadie into the tall truck, then handed her the seat belt. She buckled up and crossed her legs, looking instantly comfortable and elegant.

He sighed and went around to his side. Just as he'd expected, his knees pressed into the back of the front seat and angled toward his chest. Elegant? Not hardly.

He glanced over at Sadie. He had to admit that she looked sexy tonight. The delicious curve of her calf held his gaze a bit too long, and he quickly turned away.

Jessica turned around from her seat in the front passenger side. "We're going for pizza before the movie, Knox."

"Okay." Had Sadie known? He could only imagine the eyes that would pop at the pizza place when she walked in dressed like that.

"We'll have plenty of time to eat, don't worry."

He nodded. Well, the movie patrons would get an eyeful too. Sadie looked like she was headed to the Oscars instead of to the small theater in the mall.

Wait. He'd tuned out. What had Jessica just said the title was? That movie sounded like a chick flick.

"Sadie, I know you're going to *love* this movie. Everyone's been talking about it," his sister continued.

He bit back a groan. He really couldn't believe he'd let himself get roped into this.

"I rarely get out to movies. This is going to be fun," Sadie said with a grin.

He looked at her out of the corner of his eye. She did seem excited. He settled back in his seat and smoothed the snarky look from his face. He shouldn't ruin the evening for her, even though he was going to be miserable.

When they finally arrived at the pizza place, he unwound his long legs and stepped out of the truck, liking the fact that Sadie had waited for him to get her door. The slit in her dress exposed her leg to mid-thigh as she stepped down from the truck. Damn, she had gorgeous legs. He set his hand at the small of her back as he escorted her inside. Her waist was so small he could almost span it. That did something to him. Made him feel all kinds of protective of her.

He'd been right. Every eyeball in the place locked onto Sadie as they came in the door. He couldn't blame them. She was gorgeous all the way down to her pretty, painted toes. They headed to a booth in the back of the room, and he urged her to slide in first.

A teenaged girl had followed them to the table, and she slid menus in front of them. "What would you all like to drink?"

After they'd given their order, Jessica said, "Sadie, they have a great five-cheese pizza here, and their salad bar isn't bad, so your little vegetarian heart should be real happy."

Sadie folded her menu and smiled. "That's what I'll have, then."

Knox frowned. He'd forgotten that she was a vegetarian. It was just one more wacko thing about the New Yorker.

When the waitress came back with their drinks, Scott ordered an extra-large supreme pizza for the three of them and a small five-cheese pizza for Sadie.

Jessica patted Scott's arm. "Move over, cowboy. I'm starving, and that salad bar is calling my name."

Knox stood and offered his hand, assisting Sadie to rise.

She smiled. "Thanks. I'm hungry, and it's strange. I hadn't been hungry in weeks before I came to Texas."

He placed his hand at the small of her back and followed her. "It's this good, clean Texas air."

"Whatever it is, I'm thankful. I feel alive here for the first time in a very long time."

That got his attention. She must really have been in a bad way before coming to see Jessica.

Sadie took a plate and handed him one. Then she grabbed her tummy. "Oh! Excuse me." Leaning toward him, she whispered, "My stomach just growled!" She chuckled. "I feel so different tonight."

"You'd better get something in that belly, New York. It's on Texas time now."

She laughed. "Watch me fill this plate."

Her face seemed to glow as she moved from one dish to the next and, though he wouldn't have said it was possible, she looked even more beautiful.

Once they were all seated again, Jessica asked, "Sadie, what was your very favorite photo shoot?"

Sadie chewed, her eyes far-off and unfocused for a moment. "It would have to be when I went to the African savanna. The shoot was supposed to look like I was out in the wild, but really we were on a game reserve and inside a sanctuary. I posed with the most amazing elephant. She was used to people, and I was able to touch her and interact with her in a very special encounter. She was truly a gentle giant.

That time, after the shoot, I was actually allowed a couple of hours to go out with one of the rangers, and I saw some magnificent animals." She sighed and put her fork down. "That so seldom happens. I'm usually in and out of a place so fast I never see much of anything."

The weary sadness in her eyes touched Knox deeply, and he had an instant desire to put his arm around her. He didn't, of course.

"That sounds amazing. I'd love to get up close to an elephant like that," Jessica said.

Sadie picked up her fork. "I'll never forget it. Her eyes were so intelligent, and she was incredibly sweet with me, as if she knew that she could easily hurt me. That wonderful animal touched my soul."

She'd almost whispered the last sentence, a reverence in her voice. There was more to this East-coast woman than he'd given her credit for.

"I've always wanted to go to Africa," Knox told her. "I'd especially love to see big game. Mountain gorillas fascinate me too. I had a trip booked once but had to cancel it."

Sadie's eyes filled with interest. "I love Africa too. That sounds amazing. Maybe someday I'll actually have time to go."

Their pizzas arrived, and the rich, cheesy smell made his stomach flip-flop, despite the salad he'd just finished.

The waitress took their salad plates away as Scott said, "I don't know why I don't come here more often. I love this stuff."

Knox reached for a piece, and cheese stretched all the way to his plate. "God, this looks good." He took a big bite, and flavor exploded in his mouth. He agreed with Scott. He should make a point to get over here regularly too.

Sadie glanced at him as she picked up a piece of her own pizza. "Good?"

He patted his mouth with a napkin. "Delicious."

She took a bite of hers, and a quiet moan escaped her lips. "It's been forever since I've had pizza. The life of a model doesn't quite mesh with cheese like this."

She hadn't been hungry in weeks, and she wasn't able to eat pizza? What was her normal life like? It didn't sound good. He took another bite, savoring the meaty, cheesy flavor. His taste buds were in heaven. After swallowing, he took a long drink of his soda. Too bad this place didn't serve beer. That would have been perfect.

Scott had a ranch near Aspermont, and he and Jessica had met at a dancehall in Abilene. He put his arm around her and kissed her temple, then whispered something in her ear. She giggled.

Knox looked at Sadie out of the corner of his eye. She was watching them too. To his surprise, she looked almost sad. Why would she be affected that way? Suddenly, he wanted to know what made Sadie tick. What was behind her thoughts, her emotions? She was no longer the snooty Easterner, to be scoffed at and ignored. He wanted to get to know her. He touched her arm. "How's that pizza?"

She turned to him, and a smile masked her previous pensive expression. "Great! Just as advertised." She reached for another piece and took a bite as if to prove her point.

"Mine's amazing too. I was just thinking that I need to make it over here more. I forget this place is here."

She nodded but didn't look at him. Something had definitely come over her just now.

"So, have you heard of this movie before?" he asked.

She glanced at him. "No, I don't follow movies much, but I'm looking forward to it. Jessica says it's going to be good."

He nodded. "I'm not much into chick flicks, but I'm game."

She smiled. "Scott probably feels the same way. You guys are good sports."

She seemed more cheerful, and that made him feel better. It was surprising how quickly she'd gotten under his skin tonight.

The waitress came and put the bill in front of Scott. Knox tossed some money down, easily covering their half and more. Scott put some more on the pile, ensuring a good tip for the young woman.

"I'm too full for popcorn now, and I totally hate that," Jessica said as they stood to go.

"Me too, unfortunately," Sadie said.

She walked close to him as they made their way back to the truck, and it felt good. He helped her up into the truck and was struck again at how poised she was. Did that come from being a model? He felt like he had royalty on his arm tonight.

This being a Saturday night, the theater was busy, but they didn't have to wait in the concessions line, so they headed straight to their movie. The previews had already begun, so the theater was dark. He put his hand at Sadie's waist, steadying her as they followed the dim track lighting on the stairs to a series of four empty seats about three-quarters of the way up. He held her tighter as they crossed in front of other patrons' knees to the center of the row.

He pulled her seat down, and she settled gracefully onto it. Did the woman ever look awkward? The armrest between them was in the upright position, and he left it that way since they had no drinks to deal with. Besides, it felt kind of nice to sit so close to her.

Jessica whispered something to Sadie and she smiled.

Scott crossed his legs, the tall cowboy probably finding the narrow aisle as cramped as Knox always did. He took his hat off in deference to those sitting behind him and, a moment later, Scott did too.

The movie started a couple of minutes later and the room went black.

Sadie sighed and settled back in her seat.

Her perfume wafted over to him, slightly floral, but deeper and more intriguing. He inhaled quietly, taking it in deep. God, he loved that scent.

She crossed her legs and her dress fell open, exposing her calf and part of her thigh. His pulse picked up at the gorgeous curves he couldn't take his eyes off. He tore his eyes away and stared at the screen, but his mind made no sense of what was going on. His brain was focused on the beautiful woman beside him.

He was aware of her every move. When she uncrossed and then re-crossed her legs, he glanced her way. Not one of her sighs escaped his notice. When the sad part came, as it inevitably did in any chick flick, he watched out of the corner of his eye as she wiped away a tear. That right there surprised the hell out of him. Really touched him. It seemed so out of character for the reserved, even slightly aloof Northerner. There was a lot more to this woman than she let on.

The movie ended, and the lights came up. Jessica clasped Sadie's hand. "Didn't I tell you it was great?"

Sadie smiled. "You were right. I loved it."

Jessica looked past Sadie at him. "Well, was it torture, Knox?"

He chuckled. "I'm fine."

On the way home, Sadie looked quietly out her window. She seemed a little sad again. He wished he knew what that was all about. He needed to take her mind off whatever it was. "Why a vegetarian, Sadie?"

She turned to him and seemed to consider his question. "I guess because there's so much cruelty in the world. It's my way of helping make sure there's just a little bit less."

He turned that over in his mind. What was she talking about? It didn't really sound like she meant just animal cruelty.

"Does calf roping ever injure the calves?" she asked.

That question made sense if she was worried about animal cruelty. Calf roping was an intense sport. "You're not the first to ask me that, so I looked it up. A PRCA survey of nearly 61,000 animal performances showed that only 27 calves were injured during all that time. That's five-hundredths of one percent. So I'd say it's pretty damn safe for the calves."

She nodded, taking the information in, and he liked it that she didn't argue the point. They rode in comfortable silence the rest of the way.

At home, he and Sadie said goodbye to Scott. Knox shook his hand. "Next time, I drive, bud. My knees can't take that back seat again."

Scott laughed. "You got it."

Sadie and he left Jessica behind and walked on into the house. Sadie looked as perfect and put together as she had at the beginning of the evening. How did the woman do it?

Her bedroom door was just before his. She paused before opening it and turned to him. "Knox?"

"Uh-huh?"

"Thanks for taking me tonight. I had fun."

He smiled. "My pleasure." And he realized, despite his previous misgivings, that it was true.

Chapter Four

Sadie glanced down at her borrowed jeans. They were easily four inches too short, but otherwise they fit fine. She hadn't been able to borrow boots from Jessica because her feet were much smaller and narrower than her friend's. But she'd brought a pair of sneakers, so she'd put them on, learning from her mistake of wearing wedges to the roping the other night.

Jessica was going to give her a riding lesson this morning, and to say she was apprehensive was an understatement.

After a quick breakfast, they headed to the barn.

She brushed down Sally, the older mare that Jessica had chosen for her, proud that she had that part of the process down pat. After Jessica cleaned both horses' hooves, Sadie stood by while her friend saddled them. As she bridled Sadie's mare, Sadie couldn't help but wonder if the steel bit hurt the horse's mouth. She asked Jessica.

"No, look here, there's a space in the teeth where the bit goes, so it's comfortable for them." Jessica pried open Sally's mouth, and Sadie spotted what her friend was talking about, feeling better about the fact that she'd soon be tugging on the reins.

Jessica untied the mare. "Okay, let's head to the arena. You're good to go."

Taking the braided leather rein in her hand with a keen sense of trepidation now that the time had come, Sadie led the horse out of the barn.

Once in the arena, Jessica explained the proper way to mount, then did it herself so that Sadie could see how it was done. After dismounting again, she helped Sadie get up on her horse.

Sadie let out a relieved sigh once she was safely in the saddle. The mare had a calm disposition and stood quietly, unlike the Saddlebred gelding that had been her only previous horseback experience.

Jessica mounted again, then looked Sadie over. "Okay, sit up straight and look at your reins. Each side should be the same length. If one is longer than the other, shift it through your fingers until both sides are equal and hold it there. I chose a round rein for you because that type of rein is easier for a beginner. It's also what we use for roping."

Sadie made a minor adjustment, then nodded her head.

Jessica smiled. "You're doing great. Now, we're only going to walk today, but first things first. To turn right, you press the left rein against the mare's neck. That pressure tells her that you want to go right. Do the opposite to go left. Rein pressure does it all—at least that's what you need to know for now."

"Okay." That sounded simple enough.

"Now, to make her walk, move your hand forward and nudge her with your heels. She's a good girl. She'll mind you." Jessica eyed Sadie again. "Okay, I'll go first, then you follow me. Sally will like that."

Jessica moved her horse out at a walk, staying near the fence.

Sadie put her hand forward a few inches and tapped Sally with her heels. The old girl walked forward as if Sadie was an old hand at riding. Smiling, she told herself to relax and enjoy the experience. Her horse seemed to know exactly what to do.

Jessica looked back and nodded. Then she smiled. "You look like a real cowgirl now."

Sadie laughed. "I'll bet. But this is fun."

By the time she'd been around the arena twice, Sadie had some confidence built up. The mare had her mind on one thing: following the fence line. Sadie looked over the arena fence and out into the mesquite pasture beyond. This was wild country, beautiful in its own way.

The low roar of a heavy truck engine sounded in the drive, and Knox drove up to the barn, his gaze taking in the activity in the arena before he backed up to the feed room.

She was instantly on edge, the confidence she'd found disappearing abruptly. She examined her rein length. *Check.* She sat up straight. *Check.* Maybe she didn't look dumb.

Not long after, Knox came strolling out of the barn and up to the fence.

She didn't meet his gaze, concentrating instead on doing everything perfectly.

All of a sudden, his voice barked, "Sit up straight."

Huh? She was doing that, wasn't she? Still, she tried to sit straighter.

After a few seconds, he called, "Come over here, Sadie."

Oh, damn and blast. She tried to remember what all Jessica had said about turning and pressed the rein to Sally's neck. The horse obediently turned toward Knox, and Sadie let out a pent-up breath. When she got to Knox, she pulled back on the reins. She'd learned that skill on her photoshoot.

He'd come through the gate and was now looking up at her. "There's a right and wrong way to sit a saddle."

She nodded. "Okay."

He moved up beside her and put his hand at her hip. "Tilt forward here a bit."

She did so as tingles raced from the touch of his fingers to her core.

He took her shoulder in his hand and exerted pressure. "Your shoulders go back. Feel how these two things put a little bow in the small of your back and drive your pelvis bones into the saddle seat?"

"Yes, I do." His hand rested in the described place at her back, sending her pulse racing.

"Correct posture allows you to feel your horse's movements and your horse to feel your body's commands. It centers your mass where it needs to be so your horse has better balance." He withdrew his hand and she wanted to cry out, "No! I need more!" Somehow, his simple directions had become something sensual, sexual, an experience she would surely fantasize about.

"Keep your heels down. That means your weight's on the ball of your foot in the stirrup, where it should be." He met her gaze, and his eyes were warm. Kind, even.

Her heart did a flip-flop. "I will. Thank you, Knox. I can use all the help I can get." She patted Sally's neck, using that as an excuse to look away, afraid that her attraction was obvious.

"No problem." He stepped back a couple of paces. "Now show me how you can ride."

She urged Sally into a walk, and the mare responded beautifully. Concentrating on everything the handsome cowboy had said, she imagined that she could see herself and adjusted her seat in the saddle. The new way felt strange and stiff, but if that was correct, then she'd ride that way from now on.

"Good job!" Knox called out, and she smiled. Then she wondered when the man's approval had come to mean so much to her.

She focused intently, trying to feel her horse's movement under her. It was amazing how much more she could sense riding this way. When she looked up next, Knox was gone. The disappointment was sudden and overwhelming. Then she chided herself. The man had work to do. She stared at the place where he'd been standing and sighed. How had he gotten under her skin like this? But him helping her had been nice.

Jessica jogged up beside her and slowed to a walk. "Well, that was unexpected. My big brother never ceases to surprise me."

Sadie held back the smile that wanted to burst from her lips. "He had some good advice. I feel like I'm riding better."

"You are. Still, what was going through that guy's mind? He's usually all business."

Now Sadie did smile. If Knox helping her was really so out of character, he must like her after all.

KNOX GLANCED AT SADIE, wondering how he could feel this uncomfortable in his own damn truck. Jessica had asked him if he could take Sadie to her two doctor's appointments in Abilene since she had been called to the school by her principal to talk about a new initiative that he wanted her to head up in the coming school year.

Normally his mother could have taken Sadie, but she had an important meeting in town that she couldn't miss. So it had fallen on him, and he didn't feel as if he could have said no. Apparently, Sadie didn't drive.

Jessica had mentioned that the first appointment was for a prescription evaluation with a new psychiatrist, and the second appointment was a counseling session. She'd told him to plan to spend most of the day with her friend.

This silence was getting more uncomfortable by the minute. He asked, "So what's it like to be a supermodel? That's what you're called, right? Supermodel?"

She turned to him and smiled. "You could say that, yes. I'm one of the world's top models, but I don't let it go to my head. The fashion world is incredibly fickle. I'm the cat's meow right now, but the next big thing could happen any minute and I'd slide down that slippery slope pretty damn fast."

He frowned. What an awful way to live. "Is the pay good while you're on top?"

"Incredibly good. I save everything I can, though I do live well. I don't scrimp on help or necessities. And I enjoy my home and its view of a nearby park. I need a quiet place where I can relax when I'm not on the road." A shadow passed over her face. "I just wish that were more often."

"I'll bet the life's exciting, though."

She seemed to consider that for a moment. "It can be dangerous, I guess. I did a shoot with a tiger that the trainer assured my people was totally gentle and tame. And it was, as long as I was working with it. At the end of the shoot, though, when the trainer tried to put its collar back on, it lunged for his arm. It gave him a terrible bite before his colleague could pull it off him."

"Oh my God. You must have been terrified."

She nodded. "It really shook me." She thought a moment. "Then there was the time that I had to pose with this huge tarantula on my face. The trainer placed it so that it covered half my face, even my eye, and I had to act sexy, like everything was normal. I nearly had a heart attack, let me tell you."

Knox took his eyes from the road and stared at her. "You have got to be kidding me."

"Serious as a heart attack." She grinned. "My agency did *not* tell me about that part beforehand."

He had a whole new respect for Sadie.

"I've also swum with sharks, a whole lot of them, for a liquor ad, dressed in a flowing, full-length ball gown. That was scary as hell. And a ring of flames once set my hair on fire. That was early in my career. I wouldn't do something like that now."

He laughed. "It's hard to believe that modeling is so dangerous."

She grinned. "Believe it, cowboy."

The next silence, when it came, was a comfortable one.

He went inside for her first appointment and sat in the waiting room. She read a magazine, and as she was flipping through pages, he glanced over and noticed that she was the glamorous model in the full-page ad. "Hey, can I see that?"

She handed the magazine over. "This one's old. From last season."

"You look great, though."

She shrugged. "They Photoshop everything, you know."

"Really? It looks just like you."

She smiled. "Thanks."

It wasn't long before her name was called, and she gave him an anxious look before she stood to go.

"I'll be right here," he said, hoping to reassure her.

She gave him a tight smile and nodded.

When she came back out thirty minutes later, her eyes were slightly red, as if she might have cried. That possibility went straight to his heart. He put his hand at her waist as they walked out. "One down, one to go," he said in a cheerful voice.

"Yeah," she said quietly.

He didn't know what to say to help her feel better. He imagined baring your soul to a shrink must be miserable. He helped her up into the truck and gave her the seat belt. She wouldn't meet his gaze. Before he shut the door he said, "We've got time for a cup of coffee before your next appointment. Sound good?"

She gave him a tentative smile. "I'd love that."

There was a Jim's close by where there probably wouldn't be much of a wait at this time of day, so he headed in that direction.

Once they were seated, a waitress came by with a pot of coffee and, at his nod, filled the clean cups placed ready on the table. He loved that about Jim's. Sadie drank hers black, which surprised him.

She took a sip and stared over the brim of her cup. "So, tell me what a normal day is like for a cowboy."

He smiled. "For a cowboy or a rancher?"

"For you, Mr. Cowboy Rancher."

He chuckled. "Well, I check on cattle, feed them, put out hay. The fence mending is endless." He took a sip of his coffee. It was good and hot. The restaurant was about half full, so there was a low hum of conversation going on around them. He relaxed as he considered what else he wanted to say. "There're so many individual chores that come up every day that no day is ever the same. I might be doctoring a cow in the morning and pulling a calf in the afternoon. You've probably noticed that we don't have much in the way of hired help. For the most part, it's just me and my dad. So there's a lot of work to go around."

"You have some heavy responsibility on your shoulders." She sipped her coffee, her gaze searching his.

He nodded. "My dad's worked hard all his life. I've got plans to make things a little easier on him, though. In college I learned about ways to streamline a few of the things that we do, and even to make the ranch more profitable. Dad's kind of set in his ways, but he's open to some of the stuff I want to try."

She leaned toward him. "That sounds wonderful, Knox. I know your father must be proud of you."

"I think he is, even when he's being stubborn." He smiled. "That's part of being a Texan, I guess."

They finished their coffee and headed to her counseling appointment.

Again, Sadie looked anxious as she sat in the waiting room. He wished he could put his arm around her, give her some comfort before she had to face her demons. When her name was called, he reached for her hand and gave it a good squeeze. "I'll be right here."

When she came back through the door forty-five minutes later, her eyes were definitely red, her face puffy. He wanted desperately to take her in his arms. Instead, he rose and put his arm around her waist as he walked with her out the door. She must have needed the support. Her body leaned into him as they walked across the parking lot. Even though she was tall for a woman, probably five foot ten or so, she felt small against him.

Once they were on their way, he reached for her hand. She squeezed his fingers hard, surprising him with her strength. "You're okay," he told her, hoping desperately that she was. He realized that her being okay mattered to him now. Really, really mattered.

Chapter Five

Sadie settled deeper into the padded leather truck seat, looking out the window as the emerald wheat pasture dappled with Black Angus cattle passed quickly by. Knox's presence opposite her emanated a solid comfort. She sighed, happy to be going back to the ranch and the wonderful family who lived there. If only she'd been raised in a home like that.

"Do you miss your work, living way out in the boondocks like this?" Knox asked.

Bad thoughts came out of nowhere, swamping her burgeoning positive feeling. Without considering her words, she said, "Modeling has a very dark side. I found that out early on." She swallowed hard, deciding to tell him something that she *never* talked about, though Jessica knew. Maybe sharing with him had something to do with the fact that she'd just spilled her guts in a counseling session she'd been totally unprepared for.

She glanced at his profile. It would be easier to talk if he wasn't looking at her. "My mother pushed me into a world where people ogled my body at the age of two by entering me in a beauty pageant. Makeup, curlers, hair spray, all of that, were my usual routines as she took me on the pageant circuits. It didn't matter a bit that all I wanted to do was play."

He looked at her, his eyebrows drawn together in concern. "That's an awful way for a child to live."

"Yes, it was. My mom used me like a puppet, to make herself proud—because with her pushing me so hard and my looks, believe me, I won."

Knox's jaw clenched. "That's just terrible. Why didn't your father put a stop to it?"

"Honestly? I don't think he cared enough to stand up to my mother. She's a force to be reckoned with when she sets her mind on something, and she was bent on winning."

Sadie's stomach clenched. "Then she found modeling, and I started working the catalog scene. I was cute, so I had lots of bookings at the agency. It didn't matter that I was missing too much school and that my grades suffered. It wasn't until my mother got a visit from Children and Family Services that my mom pulled me from public school and hired a tutor to home-school me."

The black void that had lived inside her for so long opened its maw, and she forced back a whimper. "I grew fast and was tall enough and filled out enough to model adult clothing at twelve. That's when I really started making money. My mother pushed me mercilessly. Booking followed booking. When I was fourteen, she set up a shoot with a renowned photographer to update my portfolio, hoping to attract an agency overseas. It was to be an all-day thing, and she left to run errands, leaving me at his studio."

Sadie closed her eyes, blackness overcoming her. *That day. That horrible day.* She forced herself to go on. "He gave me wine. Kept urging me to drink. Refilling my glass." Clenching her hands, she said, "He raped me. I was so out of it, I couldn't defend myself. I told him no so many times, and he just ignored me."

"That son of a bitch!" Knox exploded.

She swallowed past the lump in her throat. "Of course, the shoot was over by the time he attacked me. The photos were surprisingly good. I looked much older tipsy."

"Honey, I am so, so sorry that happened to you." Knox reached over and took her hand.

"I told my mother what happened, but she wouldn't press charges. She wanted those photos for my portfolio. She told me that I'd been stupid to drink. What had I expected? Like it was all my fault."

Knox squeezed her hand so hard it hurt. "By God, it wasn't your fault! Your mother should have protected you, Sadie. Your father should have stepped up. Tell me he did!"

She shook her head. "No, he never did. It was if it never happened. That's when I learned I'd have to take care of myself. I don't drink at the social outings I'm required to attend, and I certainly don't do the drugs that are always available. And, when I turned eighteen, I got rid of my mom and started handling my own affairs. I hardly speak with my parents now, and I'm happy with that."

He increased the pressure of his hand. "Sadie, I think that's the saddest story I've ever heard. It breaks my heart."

She looked into his eyes, and the awful void began to shrink. His kindness, the concern in his gaze, sent warmth and strength flooding through her. "Thank you, Knox, for listening."

"Of course." He smiled and drew her hand a little nearer to him.

She leaned her head back, letting her gaze follow the land as it sped past—cattle with their heads down eating, ranchers driving tractors, and wild mesquite pastures hiding the wildlife living there. Old oak trees showed occasionally. They must have been growing a hundred years or more. What they must have seen since they were tiny acorns lying on the ground.

She felt better now that she'd shared her awful past with Knox. Better than she had in ages. Certainly better than she had after talking to that counselor. What was it about the handsome cowboy that could bring healing so easily to her? She closed her eyes. It didn't matter really. Knox was special. She'd just figured that out. Turning her head to the window, she let out a long sigh and smiled.

TWO DAYS LATER, KNOX pushed his breakfast plate away and looked at Sadie. "You're with me this morning."

She raised her eyebrows. "Okay?"

Jessica grinned. "I need to do some laundry anyway, Sadie."

Jeb stood up from the table. "See you all later."

"Bye, Dad," Knox glanced at Jessica, then back at Sadie. "You're getting a driving lesson." He tossed a small paperbound book on the table near her. "I picked this up at the drivers' license office in Haskell. The rules should be similar in New York." He stood and went to the sink to rinse his plate. "Study it while you're here. When you go back, get your license. In this world, you're hamstrung if you don't drive."

Her chair screeched as it scooted back. "Thank you, Knox. I haven't driven since I was a teenager. I understand what you're saying, but I don't have a car. Parking is ungodly hard to find in New York City. I have a space that comes with my flat, though."

He loaded his plate in the dishwasher and gave his mom a peck on the cheek. "Thanks for breakfast, Ma." Then he walked back to the table. "Look, I'm not saying you have to go whole-hog and buy a car. Rent one to take your test. Just get your license so that you can drive if you have to, or if you ever want to. You should have that option."

"Let me put my sneakers on." She rinsed her plate in a hurry and returned a few minutes later, ready to go.

Maddie was finishing the breakfast cleanup. "You two have fun."

"Bye, Ma." Knox put on his hat and urged Sadie ahead of him as he strode from the room.

At the truck, he had Sadie climb in the driver's side and was surprised to see that he only had to move the seat forward a couple of inches. Her sexy legs were longer than he'd expected. After a few quick instructions, he climbed into the passenger side. "Okay, start her up."

He smiled at her anxious look. "You'll be fine. Driving an automatic is easy. Be glad my truck's not a standard." The powerful engine roared to life. "Now put your foot on the brake and shift it into drive."

She complied, then pressed on the accelerator. The truck jumped ahead, whipping her head back.

Knox grabbed the dash. "Easy there. Gentle with that accelerator. It just takes a little nudge."

Sadie gave him a nervous grin. "Sorry about that. I'm more rusty than I thought."

"Just take it slow for a little while. Get your bearings. We're going to drive on one of the pasture roads while you get your legs under you."

This time, she eased down on the accelerator and the truck moved smoothly forward.

He settled back in the seat and let her drive in silence. As they neared a gate on the left for the home pasture, he said, "Turn in here."

She stepped on the brake, and his body lurched forward.

"Sorry!" she cried.

He gritted his teeth. "Just tap the brakes when you want to slow down. It doesn't take much pressure." He opened the gate, and she pulled through just fine. When he got back in the truck, he told her to follow the road that ambled along the fence line since the pasture was planted in wheat. After a moment, he said, "So I guess you didn't drive much back when you had a license?"

She glanced at him, then returned her attention to the dirt path in front of them. "Not really. We only had one car, and my dad usually had it."

Her knuckles were white as she gripped the steering wheel. She was clearly terrified. "Relax. Nothing's going to happen out here in the middle of nowhere. We'll just drive for a while." She adjusted her rear end in the seat, but her hands didn't loosen. Her long, elegant fingers had a death grip on the wheel. He kept quiet and let her drive. Experience in a safe environment where no other vehicles would challenge her was the best teacher.

He was having a hard time keeping his eyes off her. Her pale skin glowed in the sunlight. Perfect breasts swelled beneath her

T-shirt. They weren't large, but they looked just right to fill his palms. He clenched his teeth. His mind shouldn't be going there. Sadie had enough on her plate. She didn't need him lusting after her right now.

After a time, she settled further back in the seat, taking the turns easily and working the brake like a champ. He didn't give her directions. She knew what to do; her body just had to remember how.

Finally, he felt that she was ready for a real road. "Okay, let's turn around at the next gate." When they got there, he told her how to use her mirrors for a three-point turn.

Once they made it to the paved farm-to-market road, he said, "Okay, the speed limit here is fifty-five. You don't want to go too slow, or you'll be a road hazard. Look both ways carefully and, if it's clear, go ahead and pull out to the left." She was all tensed up again, and he couldn't help but feel sorry for her. He remembered back when he was learning to drive, he'd been excited, but scared to be out on the main road. He reached over and clasped her shoulder. "It's okay, Sadie. You're doing great."

She smiled grimly. "Don't let me wreck, Knox."

"Of course not. You've got this." Her hair, so dark it was almost black, brushed against the back of his hand, sending tingles racing up his wrist. With a last pat, he said, "Look, then pull out." His protective feelings were in overdrive right now. Sadie looked like she desperately needed a hug. But she eased out into the road and made it up to speed without a problem. "Perfect. Now just maintain it at fifty-five. Don't forget to look in your rearview mirror for cars coming up behind you. Always stay aware of what you're sharing the road with."

She glanced nervously in the mirror, then reached up to adjust it.

He nodded. Good for her. After several miles, her shoulders relaxed. He kept quiet, letting her get used to the feel of the truck moving at speed underneath her. Before they got to town, he said, "Pull over at that gate coming up on the right."

She braked smoothly, then pulled over and stopped.

He opened his door. "We'll switch here."

As he got behind the wheel, he glanced over at her. She climbed into the truck on her own just fine. "You did a great job, Sadie. I'll ask Jessica to take you into town in her SUV. You can practice parallel parking. That's actually the hardest part about passing your driver's test."

She rolled her eyes. "I remember."

When they got back to the ranch, he stopped at the house. "Lesson's over. You did fine."

She put her hand on the door handle, but hesitated. "Do you mind if I hang out with you for a while?"

His pulse picked up. Spend more time with this gorgeous woman? He wanted to so badly. His body responded to her in all sorts of ways, but was it a good idea for her? He studied her for a moment. She looked nervous and a little desperate. Why in the world was that? He shouldn't make her nervous. "Uh, sure. I'll just be feeding at a few pastures this morning."

She put her seat belt back on. "Great! Sounds fun."

He smiled. Fun? Only a New York City girl would say something like that. He backed up to the feed room and got out. "I need to load up some feed first."

"Can I help?"

He grinned. She was so slim she'd blow away in a dust storm. "You can try, I guess."

After opening the tail gate, he showed her the stacks of feed sacks. "I feed mostly cattle cubes. They supplement protein intake for the herds." He picked up a fifty-pound sack and headed for the truck. When he came back, Sadie was valiantly struggling to get a sack into her arms. He laughed and picked it up for her. She wrapped her arms around it like it was a pillow and walked toward the truck. He couldn't help it. He had to watch her next move.

Grinning but silent, he watched as she attempted to get the bag up into the back of the truck. She couldn't boost it high enough, and it slid toward the ground. She cried out and squatted, catching it before it hit, but was then stranded underneath her heavy burden, unable to stand up.

He laughed and went to her rescue. "Let me have that thing, woman, before you end up on your back." He took it in one arm and assisted her to her feet with the other.

She rolled her eyes. "That's a lot harder than it looks."

He patted her back, still grinning at the spectacle she'd made. "You gave it a good go. We'll find something else you can do. There's plenty of work to go around on a cattle ranch."

She stood by and watched him load the rest of the sacks, her eyes bright with interest. When he shut the tailgate, she rushed around to the passenger side and climbed in, a whole new girl from the one who had been so anxious earlier.

He looked at her from the corner of his eye as he headed to the first pasture. "I'll bet you were popular in high school, Sadie."

She grimaced. "I didn't go to high school, remember? I had tutors. I haven't stepped inside a school since I was eleven years old."

He frowned. What a terrible childhood she'd had. He'd like to tell that mother of hers a thing or two. And her father? He needed to be taken out behind the woodshed.

When they arrived at the herd, Sadie came with him to pour out the feed. "Stick close to me. Cows only care about food. They'll knock you down in a heartbeat fighting over it." She did as he said, and he was surprised at how unafraid she was. Cattle were large animals, and he and Sadie were at close quarters with them as he inspected the herd for injuries.

When they arrived at the third and final herd of the morning, while he was looking at a swollen spot on a cow's belly, Sadie did get bumped, falling into him. He caught her in his arms, shocked at how tiny her waist was and at how little meat there was on her bones. This woman needed a good Angus steak. To hell with that vegetarian shit.

She took a deep breath, her hands clutching at his chest. "Sorry about that."

He set her on her feet. "No problem." Damn, it had felt good to have her in his arms. "You okay?"

She grinned sheepishly. "Fine. I didn't move out of the way fast enough, I guess."

After he dropped her back at the house for lunch, he headed to the barn and loaded up some more feed, needing a few minutes to himself. What if he'd held her longer? Pulled her into an embrace? What would it be like to kiss her? Then he rolled his eyes. *Dream on, cowboy. That city girl doesn't give two shits about you.*

Chapter Six

The next day, Sadie leaned back in the passenger seat of Jessica's SUV, relaxed and ready for their girls' day. Her friend had called ahead and scheduled manicures and pedicures for them both, and afterwards they were headed for full-body massages at a place that Jessica raved about.

"I don't care what you say," she informed Jessica. "I'm paying for this whole outing. You're going to murder my feelings if you protest anymore. You're my host. You've giving me this fabulous Texas vacation, so you're going to let me pay today. Period."

Jessica let out a loud sigh. "If you put it that way, I guess I'll shut up."

Sadie grinned. "About time." She put her bare feet up on the dash and examined her toenails. Maybe she'd go with a beige pedicure this time. Then she asked the question that had been near and dear to her heart since yesterday. "Does Knox have a girlfriend?"

Jessica glanced over at her. "Nope. He really doesn't date much. In fact, I was surprised when he agreed to double date with me and Scott when we wanted to take you out to the movies."

"Really? But he's such a good-looking guy." Her heart raced at finding out the good news. She'd been sure there must be a beautiful woman in the picture.

Jessica grinned. "Right?" She turned back to the road. "He dated some in high school—and he even brought a girl home from college one time. But he says he has things he wants to do before he gets serious with anyone."

That was interesting. "What things does he want to do?"

Jessica shrugged. "I'm not sure of the specifics, but I know it's about the ranch. He came home from college with a lot of ideas. The ranch will be his someday."

Sadie frowned. "Wait, his? What about you?"

Her friend shrugged again. "We're lucky if the ranch can support one family. If we were to break up the ranch so I got half, no one could make a living from it. I'm okay with the plan. This ranch has been in our family since the 1800s. I don't want to see it broken up and sold."

She smiled at Sadie. "Besides, I'll probably marry a rancher, and my son will inherit his ranch."

Sadie admired the generosity behind her friend's attitude. What a wonderful family the McKinnises were. She imagined the life Knox planned for himself. A well-run, profitable ranch. A wife making a home for him, and several children to fill it. It sounded amazing. And Knox was a determined man. He'd make that dream come true.

She sighed and turned to the window. If only her life held such a lovely future. Her thoughts returned to New York and what waited for her there. Darkness slithered into her soul. She didn't want to go back.

KNOX GLANCED AT SADIE. She seemed amazingly confident while driving today. Jessica had left early this morning for a three-week training course in Dallas as the leader of the new initiative her principal was planning for the upcoming school year. Their dad had driven her to the airport. So here he was taking Sadie to her counseling appointment again.

"So do you ever have roundups like in the movies?" She glanced over at him and smiled. He liked it that she was confident enough now to take her eyes from the road for a few seconds. She was so sexy today, dressed in a white miniskirt and a shoulder-baring yellow T-shirt that hugged her body, revealing curves his eyes couldn't help but devour. Her nude, strappy heels gave her four more inches in height and made her calves look delicious.

"We do occasionally. But usually, it's the same old drill. I put out feed every day. I try to make my rounds of all of the pastures in four days. That works because I have good strong pasture grass for the cattle." He thought for a moment. "Really, it's different depending on the time of the year. During calving season, I keep a constant eye on the heifer herd. I bring the ones near calving down to the barn pasture so I can keep a close watch on them. They're the most likely to have problems during delivery. I might need to pull a calf if one of them can't have the baby on her own."

Her eyes widened. "Wow. Really? You know how to do that?"

He smiled. "Sure. I can't say that I don't have to call the vet once in a while, but I can usually help the heifer deliver safely. Of course, there's doctoring to do occasionally. Simple stuff that I can handle on my own. The bad stuff I have to call the vet out for, like that abscess the big bull had. Then I have to catch the animal up and haul it to the barn. You saw what a pain in the—" He glanced at her. "What a pain that is."

"What problems do cattle have?"

He rolled his eyes. "What don't they have? Cattle aren't very smart. They find the darndest ways to get into trouble. They eat bones and get them caught in their throat. They can die from that. They never watch where they're going, so getting cut is nothing for them. They kick each other. That causes blood pockets that can fester and abscess. Stepping on sharp stuff and going lame is another good one. Mesquite have big thorns. A downed mesquite limb is a great way for them to get a thorn between their toes or stuck in the soft part of their hoof. That's why I check the herds over when I feed them. Cattle can always find a way to mess themselves up."

"Wow. There's so much more to ranching than I ever imagined. I thought you rode horses all day."

He laughed. "That's funny. We have Hollywood to thank for that." He was actually enjoying talking about his work, and he seldom liked talking. "Then there's the inoculations, the deworming, and, of course, the bull calves need to be castrated when they're young."

She looked over at him again, and her eyes were alive with interest. The expression went straight to his heart. He turned back to the road. She'd be going home to New York soon. Being attracted to her was one thing, but getting his heart involved? That was a huge mistake.

"So why don't you tell me what *your* life is like?"

Her mouth tightened. She didn't answer right away. His question was probably a mistake. Then she said, "My life isn't like yours. My days are a blur. Nonstop travel, rushing through shoots, long, long days. Fashion shows where I have to be in and out of outfits in seconds. No rest. Parties I'm supposed to look glamorous at. Be seen with the right people. Make connections for my next job. Then home for a few precious hours or days."

She looked at him. "Compared to your life, it's absolute misery."

His jaw tightened. That's what her face looked like. Miserable. If she hated her life so much, why didn't she change it? Couldn't she do that?

"I'm so sorry, Sadie. That sounds awful."

"It is," she said quietly.

They were nearing Abilene. "Pull over at the next good place you see. I'll drive into town from here."

She nodded. After a moment, she said, "I'm saving my money. I have a nest egg. I'm going to get out someday. And I won't be another broke, has-been model with nothing to show for my time on the runway."

"Good for you."

Her voice sounded so bleak, so defeated, though her words were hopeful. She broke his heart.

A few minutes later, he was behind the wheel. "It's not far to your counselor's office. She's on this end of town."

"Really? I honestly don't remember."

When they arrived, he went in with her again. She picked up a magazine from one of the tables and flipped pages as if nothing could hold her interest. She was obviously nervous about the appointment again. When her name was called, he squeezed her hand. "You've got this."

She smiled, her eyes searching his as if for comfort, and whispered, "Thanks."

Nearly an hour later, she opened the door, and it was obvious that she'd been bawling. She looked devastated. He went into protector mode and put his arm around her shoulders as they left the office. At the truck, she could barely lift herself into the seat. He buckled her seat belt, and she didn't utter a word. She had tissues wadded up in her hand. He took them from her and handed her his handkerchief.

Her eyes filled up, and a sob escaped her. She pressed her fist to her mouth.

"Aw, Sadie." He pulled her into a hug and held her there, right in the parking lot for everyone to see. She shuddered, sniffing back tears. After a moment, he patted her back, and she settled into the seat.

As they drove out of the parking lot, instead of heading back the way they'd come, he turned right. Minutes later, he pulled up in front of Baskin-Robbins.

Sadie sat unmoving, as silent as she'd been since he'd started the truck.

He went over and opened her door. "I've never heard of anything Baskin-Robbins can't fix."

She gave him the ghost of a smile and swung her legs from the truck.

He helped her down and put his arm around her waist as they walked inside. He kept it there as they stood at the counter, giving her his strength. She leaned against him, and the gesture touched him deeply. That session had shattered her.

"I can't remember the last time I had ice cream," she said quietly and dabbed at her eyes.

He pulled her close. "Now that's a damn shame. Ice cream's the elixir of life."

That brought a tiny smile to her face. Good.

A young girl walked over. "Can I help you folks?"

He eyed the menu. "I'll have two scoops of Coffeebooty in a bowl, please."

A grin appeared on Sadie's face. "Coffeebooty?"

He laughed and pointed at the wall behind the counter. "Hey, it says it right there."

She studied the offerings, taking her time. "I'd like two scoops of Butterscotch Ribbon in a waffle cone, please."

"Good choice." He pulled out his wallet as the girl got to work on their orders.

Sadie shifted beside him, standing taller, as if she were waking from a bad dream. Knox let go of her—and instantly missed the feel of her against him. She let out a long sigh, but steadied herself easily.

When the clerk brought their ice cream, they took their treats to a table and sat down.

Sadie tasted hers. "Mmm, this is good."

He ate a big spoonful of his. It was just as great as always. "I love this place. I come here a lot."

"Really? How come you're not fat?"

He laughed. "Hey, I work it off. Didn't I just tell you all the stuff I do?"

"I guess, but ice cream's really fattening. That's why I never eat it." She took another big lick. It was all he could do not to grin, she was so obviously enjoying it. The change in her was amazing. This had been a good idea.

He took another bite. "I didn't tell you what I had to do this morning."

"What happened?"

"Remember I told you how cows eat old bones?"

"Yes?" She licked all the way around her cone to get the drips, and the sight of her little pink tongue gave him sweet shivers. Did she have any idea how sexy she was?

He yanked his mind back to his story. "I found this cow foaming at the mouth and coughing and gagging. She'd obviously swallowed something she couldn't get down." He took another bite. "So I had to go back and get my horse. Rope her and tie her to the trailer. Dad came to help, by the way. This was definitely a two-man job."

She waited for him to go on. "How did you get whatever it was out?"

"Dad did his best to hold her mouth open while I stuck my hand inside to try and feel what the hell she had stuck in there. There was something all right, wedged all the way in the back of her throat."

"What was it?"

After another bite of ice cream, he said, "I couldn't tell, but it was sure hard. I had to work like hell to get my fingers behind a corner of it, but eventually I was able to work it loose. I hooked it with a finger and dragged it out."

"Damn, Knox," she said. "What the heck was it?"

He laughed. "It was a vertebra. Probably from another cow since it was so big. We lose cattle from time to time, and the buzzards eat them."

"Oh my Lord. She was a cannibal." She drew the corners of her mouth down.

That cracked him up. "Nobody really knows why cattle love to eat bones, but my best guess is that it's for the calcium."

When they'd finished—and she *did* finish all of her ice cream—they headed back to the truck. She easily got herself up into it this time, and it did his heart good to see her so improved. When they got underway, she leaned her head back on the seat, as if her energy was all spent, then she reached for his hand. And, damn, that felt good too.

SADIE GOT UP FROM THE sofa, boredom making her nerves jangle. She was used to being so busy that she had no time to think.

Maddie popped her head into the room. "You're sure you don't want to go with me? My friends would love to meet you."

Sadie smiled. "Thanks for inviting me, Maddie. You're kind to include me. I think I really just need some time to myself, though."

Maddie smiled. "Okay, then. I'm off."

Sadie waved goodbye, feeling like the walls were closing in on her. After hearing Maddie's car drive out, she headed for the front porch and sat on the swing, setting it into brisk motion.

The horses grazed peacefully in the pasture by the barn. Cattle wandered aimlessly round the pen after finishing their morning feed. She sighed. This was such a beautiful place. It must be wonderful to live here. The motion of the swing calmed her restless nerves.

A bee buzzed at the potted flowers on the edge of the porch. She wondered if the blooms had a scent. What kind were they? She knew little about plants. Her parents had never done any type of gardening.

She drew in a deep breath. The air was so clean here. She'd never realized just how industrial the air smelled in New York City until she'd gotten a sniff of the fresh air at the ranch. Everything here was so natural—so healthy.

She closed her eyes and let her senses roam. A horse blew air from its nostrils. One of the cows in the pens *maawed* a complaint. The bee continued to hover at the blooms, gathering pollen. The muscles in her neck relaxed. In a little while, her shoulders did too.

She got up from the swing, feeling like a walk, and headed down the steps toward the barn. As she entered the big double doors, the scent of fresh hay came to her, and she sensed dust on the air. It was much cooler inside than out in the heated morning air, and she wandered back to the tack room. Inside, the smell of leather and horse made her take a deep breath. It was wonderful and earthy and she couldn't get enough of it. The saddle nearest her was intricately carved, the etched date from many years before. Jeb must have won it in a rodeo. The bridle that hung over the horn had a design on the cheek strap. She'd never realized how beautiful Western tack could be.

She wandered around, touching different objects hanging from the wall. Was that big leather collar from an old plow-horse rig? Jars of ointment sat on shelves, and she read the labels, learning their uses. A bucket held old horseshoes. Some of them had been used for hooks on the wall, and halters and lead ropes hung from them. This was a magical room.

She glanced through the door and saw a grey tabby cat, hind leg in the air as it licked its belly. She smiled and walked toward it. She'd always wanted a cat when she was growing up, but her mother wouldn't allow her to have a pet. When she came near it, the cat flopped its leg down and scooted under a stall door. She followed, and the cat sat on its haunches, staring at her.

She crouched and approached, and, to her surprise, it let her pick it up. She felt rows of nipples on its belly and guessed that it was female. The cat began to purr, and her heart melted. She rubbed her cheek against its soft head. "Who's a pretty cat, huh? You are. What's your name? Do you have a name, Miss Barn Cat?"

She went through the doors and settled into the old folding chair just outside. The cat made itself comfortable on her lap, continuing to purr loudly. Sadie's soul would have smiled if that were possible. She ran her palm down its furry back. Wouldn't it be wonderful to live here? She couldn't imagine a better place on earth to be. She inhaled, loving the natural smells surrounding her. She had on shorts, and the cat licked her bare thigh, tickling her. She grinned. If only she weren't gone most of the time, she'd love to get a cat when she got back to New York.

A gray pall settled over her, and she drew the cat to her chin. She *would* have to go back. Leaving all of this behind would break her heart. Now that she'd experienced what life could be, her job, her old life, would be that much more horrible.

An engine sounded in the distance, and she stared down the drive. It looked like Knox was approaching. A minute later, he pulled up to the barn and backed toward the feed room. He glanced at her as he stepped out of the truck, and she waved. He nodded and disappeared into the barn.

After loading a number of sacks of feed, he strode toward her. "I thought you'd be with Mom."

She shrugged, stroking the cat, who stared at Knox with her bright golden eyes. "She was sweet and invited me, but I needed some fresh air, I guess."

After a few seconds of silence, he said, "You're welcome to ride along with me, but I can't promise that it'll be exciting."

She smiled. "I'm not looking for exciting." She set the cat on the ground, and the animal looked up at Sadie in disappointment. The poor thing probably didn't get held much.

Knox opened the door for her and helped her climb into the truck. It smelled dusty and earthy, and ranching gear covered the dash. She loved it. He must have cleaned it before, when he'd taken her to her doctors' appointments.

After buckling up, she looked more closely. There was a brown vial of medicine and several syringes, plus a couple of small boxes of other medications. Some kind of brightly colored elastic wrap and papers and envelopes littered it as well. This was a working man's truck, and she now appreciated the effort he'd gone to in order to make it presentable when they'd gone into Abilene.

He glanced at her, then back at the dirt road in front of them.

"So we're going to feed some cattle, I guess?"

"Yep. I have three more herds to go today." He reached down and bumped the temperature on the air-conditioning.

It *was* getting hot. The Texas sun could get pretty brutal as the day wore on. She studied his profile out of the corner of her eye. He'd make a movie star jealous. That straight nose and strong jawline were perfect. And his shoulders looked like he lifted weights—which he did, in a way. Those fifty-pound feed sacks were as good as any weight set. His jeans looked like they'd been made just for him, they fit so well. And he wore a long-sleeved button-up shirt. That was another thing she wasn't used to. T-shirts were what she'd expected someone to wear when they worked out on a ranch. It was a casual job, after all. Was it to protect himself from the sun? Whatever the reason was, he looked amazing.

When they came to a gate, he got out to open it.

She realized that opening gates was something that she was capable of helping with. When he got back inside, she said, "I'll close it for you."

He glanced at her and grinned. "Oh, man, are you going to regret that. There's nothing a rancher loves more than to have someone ride shotgun and work the gates."

She laughed.

They spent the rest of the morning feeding. She went with him as he poured out feed in piles for the cattle, enjoying their proximity and quiet conversation about the animals while he explained what he was looking for and seeing. The simple joy being with Knox brought her drove the dread of returning to New York to the far corners of her mind.

They returned to the ranch house for lunch, where she helped him make sandwiches as Maddie was still at her charity function.

As they ate, Knox said, "I have to get a load of feed this afternoon. Want to ride along? It'll take the rest of the day."

Her pulse picked up speed at the idea of spending more time with the handsome man. The morning had been amazing, and she didn't want their time together to end. "I'd love to go. Thanks for asking."

He nodded. "Great. We're going to Gorman. There's a mill there where I buy my feed wholesale."

"That sounds like a good deal."

"It is. Feed's expensive, but I have to give it to the herds to improve their protein intake. It's worth the drive to get it wholesale."

When they'd finished lunch, he hooked up the trailer to the truck and they headed out. "It's a nearly two-hour drive, so settle in and get comfortable. I haul as much weight as the trailer can carry when I go."

She leaned back against the seat and relaxed. "Sounds good. You know I have nothing better to do." She looked out the window at the grass pasture passing by. "Texas is so beautiful."

He glanced at her and smiled. "I think so, but then I grew up here. Some people would disagree that this country is beautiful. They like land with water and lots of green lawns and houses everywhere you look." He shook his head. "Not me. I like it here. The wildness. The mesquite with its thorns. Even the cactus has its place. This land has strong grass—nutritious. It makes for healthy cattle when you can get enough of it." He sighed. "I love this part of Texas."

She bit her lip. How wonderful it would be to have that contentment with your life. What an amazing gift. Her life was a million miles from what he described.

"You're so lucky to have the life you do. The ranch is absolutely amazing."

He smiled. "Thanks. I think so."

She looked out the window, letting her mind roam, but keeping it far away from her own life, from her job. From anything that reminded her of the future.

When they got to Gorman, she was amazed at the sight of the huge feed mill. The tall silos and massive buildings looked weathered, like they'd been there for long years. Knox pulled into the parking lot of a small building across the street.

He looked over at her. "I'll just be a few minutes." When he got out, he left the truck running so that the air-conditioning would keep her cool.

Over at the mill, she couldn't see anything happening. Another truck was backed into what looked like a huge covered loading dock, but she didn't see anyone around. She wondered what kinds of feed they made there. A big semitruck pulled up in front, and the driver got out and walked inside an open door in the building.

Ten minutes later, Knox opened the truck door and climbed back in. "They'll load me in a few minutes. We're next."

Then she noticed that two young men were loading feed into the truck that was backed up to the loading dock.

Knox glanced at her. "Cool enough?"

She nodded. "Fine. Is it hot out there?"

He rolled his eyes. "Yep. It'll be even hotter later."

When the other truck drove out, Knox pulled forward, though he didn't try to back into the small dock. One of the guys came over and looked at the ticket Knox held out the window, then nodded.

"This'll take a while." Knox settled back in his seat, and Sadie heard and felt the regular thump of feed sacks being tossed into the trailer. "Tomorrow, Eddie'll come out to the ranch and unload the feed. That's a job I don't have to do myself anymore, thank God."

She raised her eyebrows. "Eddie?"

"He's a high school kid who helps out once in a while. It's handy to have someone we can call when we need an extra hand. He's a good kid. His family lives half-way to Old Glory on a small place, and he's always looking to earn a few bucks."

Eventually the sacks of feed were loaded and Knox slowly pulled out of the parking lot. "We'll drive slower on the way home with this load behind us."

They were quiet as Knox drove, each lost in their own thoughts. She relaxed into the comfortable seat, at peace. Happy to be with the kind, handsome man opposite her and, for the first time in memory, happy to be alive.

As they approached the intersection with I-20, Knox asked, "Hungry?"

Surprised, she realized that she was, even after having lunch just a few hours earlier. "Oh, I could definitely eat."

He smiled. "Great, there's a good little place coming up. I usually stop there when I come for feed."

Right at the intersection, Knox pulled into the parking lot of a small mom-and-pop diner. "You're going to love this."

She smiled and opened her door. "I can't wait."

When they got inside, they found an open table, and Knox held her chair for her. She loved that he did that so often. Were all Texas men such gentlemen, or was Knox just special that way?

An elderly woman brought their menus. "Iced tea for you both?"

Sadie grinned. Iced tea should be the state drink, Texans liked it so much. "I'd love some."

Knox nodded and opened his menu.

She opened hers too. The number of fried foods on offer boggled the mind. She loved this place! Now that she wasn't worrying about calories, her mouth watered as she considered what to order. After a moment she grinned and closed her menu.

Knox looked up. "That was fast."

"I'm hungry."

He laughed and shut his. "Me too."

The waitress must have noticed because she came right over. "Ready?"

"I'll have the macaroni and cheese and your house salad with ranch dressing, please." Just saying it made Sadie feel deliciously gluttonous.

"And I'll have an order of fries and more ranch dressing to dip them in." Guilt instantly washed through her, but she threw it out just as fast.

"Sure thing, hon."

Knox ordered his hamburger and fries, and the woman walked away.

"Wait until you see their hamburgers. They're amazing," he said.

Her stomach growled, and she clutched it and grinned. "I can't believe how hungry I am right now."

"You need a good feed-up, New York. A strong wind could blow you away."

She rolled her eyes. "No way. And I don't know what I'm going to do about my weight when I leave, but I'm totally not worrying about that now." And she wouldn't. She promised herself that.

Her meal, when it arrived, was as fabulous as she'd hoped. She wasn't able to eat all of it, as the portions were huge. Knox had been right. This place was amazing.

Knox looked over at her and smiled when she pushed her plate away. His eyes were warm, and there was something else there that set her pulse racing. "Looks like you found something you liked."

She patted her tummy. "Oh my God. I wonder if they make macaroni and cheese like this in New York City?"

He laughed. "I don't know. Maybe I'll have to ship you some when you go back." His eyes darkened, and he looked away. Was he sad that she'd be going back? Did that mean that he cared about her? Because today had made her realize something. She cared about this handsome cowboy now. There was no denying it.

When they got back on the road, he glanced over at her. "You're welcome to tag along with me tomorrow, if you like. I'll be working on the ranch all day."

The corner of his mouth tilted up and her heart did a flip-flop. Maybe he'd enjoyed this day together just as much as she had. She smiled. "I'd love that."

Chapter Seven

Knox bent and gave his mom a kiss on the cheek, noting that Sadie had appeared for breakfast dressed in her New York jeans and sneakers, ready for their day together. Why in the hell did people think that big holes in their jeans looked cool? He'd never figured that one out. He nodded at her. "Good morning."

"You look nice today," his dad said.

Sadie smiled. "Thank you, Jeb." She sat at the table and glanced at Knox. "I'm excited about today."

He chuckled. "Nothing exciting about ranch work."

"I've packed a lunch for you two," Maddie said. "I'll be gone all day."

"Thanks, Ma." He sat across from Sadie and took a bite of the sausage patty that was calling his name. His mom made the best breakfasts.

"I heard from Jessica last night. The training's going well, but she's sick of living in a hotel room," Sadie said.

"I'd hate that too." Knox glanced up from his plate. How could Sadie look so beautiful with so little effort? Her hair was in a ponytail and, even with barely any makeup on, she still looked gorgeous this morning. He picked up the cap he'd brought for her from the chair beside him and tossed it on the table. "You'll need this today."

She put it on and grinned. "Thanks!"

After breakfast, they headed out to the truck. She climbed in and buckled up before he could help her, and he smiled at her eagerness. He'd bet she would lose that enthusiasm after a long day in the heat. Before breakfast, he'd loaded the feed they'd need into the truck, so they headed straight for the west pasture. After locating the herd, he slowed to a stop. "Stick with me, New York. I don't want you getting stepped on."

She smiled. "Got it, cowboy."

He chuckled and got out to grab a bag of feed. The cattle heard him rip the top off and gathered around the truck, eagerly milling around. "Back up, now!" he yelled, and pushed at a few of them. They stepped away, but didn't move far.

Sadie had moved up next to him and stayed right by his side as he poured out pile after pile of cattle cubes. The cows jostled each other in their eagerness to reach the food. Sadie's arm brushed his, and a shiver of attraction rippled through him. Having her this close, he could smell her perfume. Who wore perfume for a day on the ranch? But he loved it that she had.

He shook the last cubes from the bag. "Let me look them over for a minute, then we'll go." He'd already checked out a few of them as he fed, but with Sadie close at his side, he walked through the herd.

"Do you see anything wrong?" she asked as she kept up with him.

"Not yet. Usually, I don't." He shoved at a cow's hip, and she swung toward him, picking up her hind hoof as if she were going to kick, then thumping it down again. He smiled at her antics.

He finished his inspection, and they headed back toward the truck. He felt Sadie's absence immediately as she made for the passenger side—like a warm spot had suddenly turned cold. Damn, it was great having her along today. He'd never realized how lonely his days were until Sadie had begun accompanying him.

She slammed her door. "Where to next?"

"Same old thing. Feeding at another pasture."

"Great!"

He chuckled. Who'd have thought that feeding cattle could be fun?

They went through the same process with the next herd, and his senses were on high alert with the beautiful woman by his side. Instead of being irritated by her questions, he looked forward to the sound of her low, sexy voice. The women he'd known in the past had higher-pitched voices that easily got on his nerves. Sadie's was rich, sweet, soothing.

By lunchtime, he wanted to take her in his arms and find out what kissing those full lips would be like. Of course, he wouldn't. He hoped that she didn't realize how attracted he was. She'd appeared to enjoy every minute of their morning, though her cheeks were a little flushed from the heat of the day. The temperature was in the nineties already, and it was just past noon. Late August was one of the hottest times of the year in Texas.

"I wasn't going to head to the house for lunch since Mom packed one for us, but it's hot. Why don't we go back and hang out in the air-conditioning for a while?" He examined her face again. Oh yeah, it was definitely a good idea.

"That sounds great. I'm about to melt." She took off her cap and wiped her forehead.

They ate in the cool kitchen and drank cold iced tea from the fridge.

Sadie kept looking at him and smiling. He'd never seen her act so happy. "If you're tired, you don't have to go out this afternoon. I'll be going over one of the fence lines and making repairs. It'll be boring as hell."

"I'm game. Don't worry about me." She looked as eager as she had this morning.

He nodded. "Fine with me. We'll take some cold water in the cooler. That sun's going to bake us."

He'd be checking fence in the south pasture today. When they went out again, he pulled along the fence from the gate, driving slowly, examining the wire for sagging or downed strands and broken or bent posts or stays. Everything looked fine for a while, but then he spotted a broken top strand. He slowed to a stop and got out.

Sadie opened her door too. "What's wrong?"

"Some deer probably got caught in the top strand. It's broken." He went over and took a good look. "Yeah, there's blood and fur on one of the barbs."

"Did the animal get hurt?"

He glanced at her. "Probably not badly. Don't worry." He reached for some baling wire and two pairs of work gloves in the back of the truck as Sadie shadowed his footsteps. At the fence, he picked up one side of the downed strand and handed it to her. "Hold this. I'll have you pull it tight in a minute." He grabbed the other end and twisted the baling wire onto it, tying it off snugly. He glanced at Sadie. "Okay, tug on your end as hard as you can—and watch out for the barbs."

She pulled, and he almost laughed when she let out a grunt with her effort. He quickly tied off the baling wire to the end of the strand. "Okay. Let go."

She gasped and released it. The strand was nice and tight. She said, "Wow, that's amazing."

He chuckled. "Tricks of the trade. Let's go." They started off, driving slowly again. Normally he walked, carrying the loppers and nipping small cactus and little mesquites sprouting in the fence line or the pasture drive, but he didn't think that Sadie could take the heat of being outside. The most important thing was making sure that the fence was sound, so that's what they were doing today. The air-conditioning in the truck would keep her cool while they drove.

Soon Sadie said, "I think I see something."

"You sure do. We need to tighten up that strand." He slowed to a stop. This time, all he needed were his pliers. When they got to the trouble spot, he said, "Here's how we do this." Taking the strand, he grasped it with his pliers and twisted it into a Z shape, then pinched it together. The strand was instantly tighter. He did this several times until the wire was taut.

"That's a neat trick," Sadie said.

"Works like a charm." He shoved his wire cutters in his pocket. "Come on. We've got a lot of fence line to cover."

The next problem they found would be harder to fix. "Looks like a hog busted through here." Feral hogs were a huge problem in Texas, and they were incredibly destructive. They dug up his pasture grass and did damage just like this to fence lines. He pulled some more baling wire from the truck and glanced at Sadie. "Need you to hold the wire again. Can't believe there's three strands down."

While she was struggling to hold the second strand, she suddenly cried out.

He dropped his pliers and reached for her. "What happened?"

She hadn't let go of the strand, though her face was full of pain. "I think my nail bent back. It hurts like hell."

"Drop the damn wire. Let me look at it." How bad was it? He couldn't stand it that she was hurt.

She removed her glove. Her finger was bleeding, the nail torn most of the way off and dangling by an edge.

She sucked in a breath. "Damn."

He took out his pocketknife. "I need to remove it. Hold still now."

He glanced at her as he opened the knife. She had a tense but resolute look on her face. His protective feelings were running rampant. With a delicate touch, he grasped the broken nail, then nipped it off.

Sadie let out a gasp but didn't cry out. The nail bled some more, and he gave her his handkerchief.

She held up her palm. "Oh no, I couldn't. It'll ruin it."

He pressed it into her hand. "I have plenty of them. Take it. Wrap it good, now." She was a tough one. Those nails were thick. What did Jessica call them? Solar nails? It must have hurt like hell to break one off past the quick.

"I heard Mom say that she's going into Abilene for groceries tomorrow. Why don't you ride along and get this fixed? I'm sure she'd be happy to have you." He picked up his pliers again and started working on the fence. "You take a break. I'm used to doing this by myself."

She leaned over and gave him a quick kiss on the cheek. "Thanks for fixing me up."

He nearly dropped his pliers as a rush of heady attraction sped through his body. It was all he could do to keep from pulling her into his arms.

She tucked her glove into her pocket. "No, I can help. I'll just be careful." She grasped the wire, using her other fingers, and his admiration for her increased. That nail had to be hurting badly.

Soon they were back in the truck. He reached into the back and pulled out a bottle of cold water from a cooler. "Drink this. You'll dehydrate easily in this heat." He got one for himself and drank long swallows. After that kiss of hers, he was hot from more than the sun.

By four o'clock, Sadie's face had flushed dark pink and her strength was flagging badly. He called it a day and headed back to the house early.

She removed her cap as they bumped over the pasture road. "There's really an art to fence-mending, you know?"

He chuckled. "Art? Not hardly. Just long years of practice."

"No really, I mean it. It's quite a skill. Something that you learn, passed down from one generation to the next." She looked so earnest that it went straight to his heart.

"You're right, I guess. I learned it from my dad, and he learned it from his." It was nice that she recognized the hard work that went into keeping up with a good fence. That was an important part of ranching.

He pulled up to the ranch house a few minutes later.

Sadie turned to him before she opened her door. "Knox, I had an amazing time with you today." A smile lit up her face and sent tingles racing from his belly to his brain. This beautiful woman was getting to him—and in a big way.

"Thanks for coming with me. It was nice to have company." And he really meant that. It had been something to remember having her with him today.

She grinned impishly. "Being a cowgirl is hard work."

He smiled back. "You're going to be a good cowgirl someday. Don't worry."

He headed to the barn, needing to feed the horses and cattle, but more than that, needing some time alone to process his feelings. He was full-on attracted to Sadie and, with the prospect of her leaving soon, it was such a bad idea. The thing was, he didn't know what to do about it. An image of her beside him today flashed before him. Damn, she was hot. And he wasn't talking about the sun.

"THANKS FOR ALLOWING me to tag along." Sadie glanced over at Maddie as they headed to Abilene the next morning. Knox's mom had been happy to have Sadie along and knew where the salon was that Jessica used.

"Of course, dear. Actually, I was hoping that we could talk." She took her eyes from the road, and met Sadie's gaze. "Knox doesn't date much. Do you know that?"

Sadie's heart began to pound. What was this about? "Jessica said something about that."

"Really?"

"Yes."

"Sadie, you're going to be going home soon. That's right, isn't it?" Maddie's smile was reassuring.

"Yes, I have to be back for the spring fashion show in September. Why?" There surely was a point to this conversation.

Maddie kept her attention on the road. "Honey, my son may seem like this strong, confident young man that nothing can hurt." She glanced at Sadie. "But he can be hurt. Just promise me that you'll be careful, okay?"

Sadie nodded. "I will, Maddie."

Sadie kept quiet for the rest of the way into Abilene, then helped Maddie do the grocery shopping. Sadie couldn't believe how big the H-E-B superstore was. New York City had nothing to compare to it.

When they arrived at the salon, she had the technician take her nails down short.

On the way back to the ranch, Maddie chatted as if the awkward conversation had never happened. Sadie was happy to let the topic rest, but she wondered, would Maddie's obvious concern about her son come between her and Knox?

THAT EVENING, SADIE set the last plate on the dinner table as Maddie put the bowl of brussels sprouts in the center.

Knox walked into the room, and immediately noticed her nails. "Looks like you got that nail fixed, but aren't they all a lot shorter?"

Sadie smiled. "I figure if I'm going to be a cowgirl, I'd better be prepared. No more long nails."

He nodded. "Well, good for you. So you're coming out with me tomorrow, then?"

"Sure am."

She loved the quick smile he gave her. "Fair enough."

After dinner, Sadie asked Knox, "So, what's on the agenda for tomorrow?"

He went to the fridge and took out two beers. "I think that conversation calls for a drink." He handed one to her. "Come on."

She followed him out to the front porch, where he sat down in the swing and patted the seat beside him.

Her pulse picked up as she settled in next to the handsome cowboy. Did he have any idea how he affected her?

He took a swallow of his beer. "Tomorrow will be more of the same. Feeding cattle. Unless I find one of them injured, that is. I'll have to take care of something like that right away."

"That would be interesting. Not that I'm hoping an animal gets hurt."

He chuckled. "Usually, it's something I can take care of easily."

"You sure keep yourself busy." She took a swallow of her beer. "Do you and your dad coordinate what you do around the place?"

"Yes. We usually talk on the weekends and make a game plan. Then he does his thing and I do mine, unless something comes up that takes more than one person, like catching up a lame cow."

His large, muscular body filled more than half of the swing. Her body responded with a rush when his scent—his masculine cologne and a faint hint of perspiration from the hard work he'd done that day—accosted her. It was intoxicating, and she didn't want to think of the conversation with Maddie. She wanted to imagine his arms around her, his firm lips on hers.

He stretched his arm along the back of the swing and settled his other on the armrest. She felt immediately as if he was holding her close. "So, tell me what you like to do for fun."

Well, that was easy. She said, "I never have time for fun."

He raised his eyebrows. "That can't be true."

She shrugged. "There are some social things that I have to attend. But after being attacked, I don't let myself relax when I go to events."

His eyes widened.

"If anything, I have a soft drink and leave as quickly as I'm able." She paused. "I guess the thing I most enjoy is spending time at home. That just doesn't happen very often." She took a sip of beer. "I learned to depend on myself, and I make sure that my life stays in focus."

He set his beer on the porch and reached for her hand. "I'm sorry that your mom was so awful."

She nodded as tingles raced up her arm from his clasp. "Me too. I've often wondered what my life would be like if I'd been raised in another family."

He squeezed her fingers. "What's your mother doing now that she's not managing your career?"

"I don't really give a damn." She took a long swallow of beer as if to rinse a bad taste from her mouth.

They swung in silence for a while, Knox keeping the swing going with little pushes.

A gentle breeze blowing in from the pasture lifted a lock of her hair, and it tickled her cheek. She was drawn to this quiet, sometimes brooding man. Holding his hand felt like heaven.

Sadie wanted to get closer to him, even though she had nothing in common with the handsome cowboy. It felt like she'd been looking for this man, this straight and true brother of her best friend, all of her life.

She let out a long sigh, and he looked at her and smiled. "Guess I'd better turn in. Work starts early in the morning."

She nodded. "I'll be ready."

He squeezed her hand one last time and stood to go.

As he walked away, he took a big part of her peace with him. She needed him now, and somehow that felt okay.

Chapter Eight

Knox turned the truck around and headed out the ranch drive. Sadie was dressed in the way-too-short jeans that she'd borrowed from Jessica. He smiled. He was going to do something about that today.

When they got to the farm-to-market road, Sadie said, "I thought we were working on fence today?"

"I changed my mind. We're going into Abilene this morning. We'll work on fence after lunch."

"Okay." She kept looking at him as if expecting an explanation, but he wanted their destination to be a surprise.

She told him about her phone call with Jessica the previous evening, and he was happy to hear that things were going well with his sister. But really, he was having a hard time keeping his thoughts off how sexy Sadie looked.

He bit back a groan. Why did he have these thoughts? Sadie was just here temporarily. She'd probably never thought of him as anything but her best friend's big brother. It was crazy to imagine kissing her. Making love to her. But that was just what had happened as he'd lain in bed last night. He'd had all kinds of lusty thoughts. If only Sadie were one of Jessica's other friends instead of a model from New York City, things would be so simple. He could take her out on dates, even fall in love with her if that were in his future.

"Knox? Did you hear me?"

"Huh? No, I'm sorry."

"I said I appreciate it that you let me tag along with you nowadays. I'd be bored to tears if you didn't."

He glanced at her. "My pleasure." Her smile did something to him at an elemental level. His heart raced, his chest felt tingly, and he needed more air, somehow. He'd come to depend on spending his days with her. Needed her with him. If he let himself think about her leaving, fingers of fear slithered around in his belly. What would it be like when she went back east again?

They entered the outskirts of Abilene, and it didn't take long to arrive at their destination.

"A Western store?" Sadie said, her brows raised in surprise.

"Yep, come on inside. If you're going to be a cowgirl, you need to look like one." He grinned as he stepped from the truck. This was going to be fun.

When they walked inside, a young woman approached. "Welcome. Can I help you with something?"

"Sure can. This is Sadie." He clapped her on the shoulder. "She needs two pair of Wranglers, some ranch boots, a belt, a couple of long-sleeved shirts with UV protection, and a hat."

The sales associate eyed Sadie a moment as if to assess her size. "Let's go look at a few things. We'll fix you up."

Soon, the two women disappeared into the fitting room with bundles of clothing over their arms. Knox smiled. He couldn't wait to see Sadie. She'd looked so excited as the other woman had held up clothing to her to check the look and fit.

A few minutes later, the associate came out, then returned with different jeans. The others must not have fitted. He paced the aisles, imagining Sadie changing clothes. Did she wear matching panties and bra? He sighed and rolled his eyes. He should kick himself for that thought.

He went over and took a look at the hats they had in stock, wondering what size her head was. He'd sure get a kick out of seeing her in one.

"What do you think, Knox?"

He turned to see Sadie striding down the aisle leading to the changing rooms, strutting like it was a fashion runway. She drawled, "I'm a Texas girl now."

He laughed out loud. "You look great!"

And she did. More than great. Sexy as hell.

"Now you need some boots and a hat."

The sales associate arrived a moment later with several pairs of boots. "I'm sorry, we don't have them in narrow. Those are special order. But if you wear thick socks, these might work." She led Sadie to the nearby seats and squatted in front of her, opening the first box.

"Can I see all of them first before I choose?" Sadie asked.

"Sure thing." The young woman opened the boxes and set them on the floor in front of her.

"Knox, which ones do you like?" Her eyes gleamed with excitement.

"It's up to you. Why don't you pick the most comfortable ones? They all look nice." He was enjoying the hell out of this. Sadie looked so happy.

She finally settled on a medium-brown, square-toed boot that would wear well. It was a good choice. She left the boots on instead of putting them back in the box.

The associate took a good look at Sadie's head, then walked off, returning with a hatbox. "Try this on for size."

Sadie did. It was a little big, so the young woman soon returned with several more boxes. "These should be right. Go look in the mirror. Figure out which one you like."

"Okay." She turned to Knox. "You have to help me with this. I'm clueless."

He smiled. "Okay." In the end, he chose the Resistol hat for her.

She turned her head side to side, getting the hat in full view. "This is so awesome. I look like a real cowgirl."

He laughed. "Yes, you do." He carried the hatbox for her as they headed up to the register. She grabbed the clothes she'd worn to the store, which the sales associate had put in a bag for her.

The young woman carried the other shirt and pair of jeans to the front and began ringing up their purchases. Knox reached for his wallet.

Sadie held up her hand. "No way! My clothes. I'm paying."

Knox shook his head. "My idea. *I'm* paying."

Sadie was quicker. She tossed her credit card down. "I am *not* letting you pay for all of this, Knox. I love it that you brought me here so that I can finally dress appropriately, but that doesn't mean that you have to pay for it. Just getting me here is gift enough." She threw her arms around his neck and kissed his cheek, hard. Then kissed it again.

He froze for a second, shocked, then wrapped his arms around her. She felt so damned good. "You're welcome, then." He didn't want to let her go.

She stepped back and smiled brilliantly up at him. "This was so fun. Thank you."

She hooked her arm in his as the sales associate handed her her purchases. "I'll let you buy me lunch, though."

His body, already on fire from her hug and kiss, responded to her touch. He was afraid to even imagine what the front of his jeans looked like. "You're on, New York." Even if he'd wanted to, one thing was clear. He could never tell this woman no. Not about anything. He was hers now.

SADIE CLIMBED INTO the truck as they left the Western store, still buzzing from the kiss she'd given Knox. She'd meant it as a friendly thank-you, but it hadn't felt that way at all once she'd slipped her arms around his neck. Her libido had raced into overdrive, her body responding with fire racing through her core. She'd wanted to follow up that chaste kiss with a long, slow, sensual taste of the sexy man's mouth—something that she knew could never happen.

Knox put her purchases in the back seat before climbing in his side. "I've got to stop by the tractor place, then how about an early lunch?"

"Sounds great." His handsome profile set her pulse racing, so to distract herself she asked, "What do you need to do at the tractor store?"

He glanced over at her, and his eyes did something to her. Something good. They glowed with interest. Was he attracted to her too? "I need some parts for my John Deere 8360."

John Deere? What was that?

He must have seen her confusion because he said, "John Deere makes the green tractors that you might see out in the fields around here. We have two—one's a 2013 model 8360R."

"Oh. Where are your tractors? I haven't seen them yet."

"Sometimes they're at the barn, but right now they're both in fields out on the ranch." He smiled. "It's not like we have to keep them in a garage or anything."

Once at the tractor place, the man at the long counter greeted Knox like an old friend. After they shook hands, Knox rattled off the things he needed and the man headed into the large back room filled with shelf after shelf of parts, large and small. When he returned, his arms were loaded. "You've got your work cut out for you," he told Knox as he set everything down.

"I should have gotten around to some of it a long time ago. I'm playing catch-up now."

When the man rang up the total, she was shocked at the price. Fixing tractors wasn't cheap.

As Knox turned to go, she reached out her hands. "Let me help with some of that."

"Thanks." His warm smile sent tingles racing through her.

Back in the truck a few minutes later, he asked, "What sounds good for lunch?"

She shrugged. "As long as I can find something without meat, I'll be happy."

He thought for a moment. "Can you eat at a Chinese buffet?"

"Sure. I'll figure something out."

The buffet was near the tractor store, and a few minutes later, they were making their way through the line of customers already at the food bar.

"So, what do you think you can eat?" Knox asked as he dished an entrée onto his plate.

"Well, the steamed rice, for sure, and there're stir-fried mushrooms and steamed veggies coming up. Oh, and Szechuan green beans. I love those." Her shoulder brushed his, and goosebumps raced down her arm. She was so damned attracted to the man. His tall, strong body drew hers like a magnet as they took slow steps through the line.

She spied some vegetable spring rolls and nabbed a couple, then grinned as Knox brushed past her to find a table. His plate was heaped with food. After grabbing a cup of hot and sour soup, she joined him.

A waitress stopped by and took their order for two iced teas.

Knox smiled. "Looks like you found plenty to eat."

She loved that grin of his. Everything about the man was turning her on. Dang it. She needed to get hold of herself. "Sure did. Coming here was a good idea."

He dug into his food like a starving man. The guy obviously loved his Chinese food.

She grinned and started on hers. She couldn't remember the last time she'd felt like this. Happy, carefree, open to the world around her. What would it be like to feel like this all of the time?

Later, as they drove home, she settled back in her seat, full and a little drowsy. She glanced over at Knox. He had one wrist on the steering wheel, relaxed, and leaned on the door's armrest. She loved his smile when he was peaceful like this. And he had such beautiful teeth. She was a teeth person. She liked good, strong, white teeth in a man, and Knox's were perfect.

They didn't talk for a while, and she kept an eye out the window after they got out on the highway, hoping to spot one of the green tractors. Then, on a whim, she reached out and clasped his hand that now lay on the center console.

His head whipped around, and his gaze met hers.

She said, "I enjoyed today. Now that I'll be dressed for the part, I can really be your cowgirl."

He raised his eyebrows, and a devilish look appeared in his eyes. "*My* cowgirl?"

She grinned and let his question hang in the air. A moment later she said, "Jessica told me that she's working hard at her training, but that she's really excited at all of the possibilities for the new school year." She bit her lip. "She said that she misses me, and I miss her too. It's lonely with her gone so long."

His hand tightened around hers. "Let's go out to dinner tomorrow. Getting away for the evening will be good for you."

Her heart fluttered. Did he want to spend time with her, or was he just being nice?

"That sounds wonderful, Knox. Thank you for asking." His hand was warm, and she felt like a part of his strength passed to her through it.

He nodded and talked about needing to buy a new bull for one of the herds and about a very young heifer that had been accidentally bred by her sire that he was worried about.

She told him about her flat and that it overlooked a park and how much she loved being there when she wasn't traveling. She realized that she had relaxed completely. That never happened. She'd struggled with anxiety for years. She squeezed his hand. "You're good for me, cowboy. I think I may be able to sleep when I go to bed tonight."

He laughed. "Wait, I make you sleepy? That's not exactly what a man wants to hear from a sexy woman."

She grinned. "You think I'm sexy?"

He gave her a lazy grin. "Sadie, you're hotter than a habanero pepper, and that's saying something."

She laughed and turned to her window. Knox was as handsome as the devil himself—and she was finding it impossible to resist him.

FRIDAY NIGHT, KNOX glanced over to where Sadie sat under the oak tree. He gestured at Blake and walked over to the roping box. They were on break after roping the first pen of calves, and he wanted to talk to his friend before Sadie came over.

Blake came up and slapped him on the back. "What's up, bud?"

Knox wasn't exactly sure how to begin. "Um, you know that Jessica's been out of town, right?"

Blake narrowed his eyes. "Yeah, so?"

Knox sighed. "So, Sadie's been hanging out with me. She rides around the ranch with me while I feed. I've been taking her into Abilene for her appointments." He couldn't quite meet his friend's eyes. "I guess, well—I like her, Blake."

"Is that a problem or something? I don't get it. Damn, boy, she's gorgeous. I'd be over the moon if I was you."

Knox looked at him. "The problem is, she came here because things weren't good for her back in New York. She was having a real rough time of it. She's like, one of the best models in the whole world. She's under incredible pressure." He shook his head. "Me getting involved with her might really mess her up."

Blake glanced in the direction of the oak tree, then back at Knox. "Look, Sadie's a grown woman, and she sure seems like the kind of person who knows her own mind. I don't think she'll do anything that she doesn't want to. Let her decide. I'm sure you'll do that, right?"

Knox gave that some consideration. Of course he wouldn't push himself on her. What Blake said made sense. "Right. That's not me."

Josh called out, "Sadie, how you doing tonight?"

Knox saw Sadie wave to his friend and grimaced, then pushed away from the roping box and slapped Blake on the back. "Thanks, bud. I appreciate it."

Knox pulled a beer from his ice chest and joined the other guys.

Sadie smiled at him as she walked up to them. "You're doing great this evening."

He moved next to her, feeling his body respond immediately with a wave of excitement. "Thanks. The calves seem to be cooperating tonight."

The other guys chuckled.

Ryder said, "Not for me. I suck."

Everyone laughed and, as they continued to talk, the conversation faded into the background as Knox's attention became focused on the beautiful woman beside him. She wore a short white skirt and matching tank top, a perfect outfit on this warm Texas evening. She took a sip of wine, and the muscles of her throat worked as she swallowed. He somehow found that so sexy. He wanted to take her in his arms, to hold her close, to feel her body mold against his. He wanted more than to just talk, to just ride together in his truck. Wanted to be more than just friends.

"Knox?"

"Huh?"

"I was talking about the Memorial calf roping back in June and the saddle you won. You using it, or is it just a trophy?" Ryder asked.

Knox grinned. "Now why would I go and use a beautiful thing like that out on the ranch?"

"You won a saddle?" Sadie asked.

Knox nodded. "It's one of the fancy ones hanging in the tack room. Take a look next time you're in the barn."

"Oh, I noticed one by the door but it looked kind of old. How cool is it that you won a saddle, though?" She grinned as if he was a movie star and hooked her arm through his. Damn, was that all it took to win her over?

He smiled. "It's not that special. They gave six away that day."

The other cowboys laughed. "Come on, man. It's great to win one. Admit it."

Knox kicked some dirt, feeling a little bit uncomfortable. "Yeah, it felt pretty good, I guess."

"Well, if you feel bad about winning it, you can go ahead and give it to me, bro," Blake said.

Knox shoved his friend's shoulder and laughed.

The guys joked and teased with Sadie while they finished their beers, and Knox had to tamp down on a sudden flush of jealousy. He was being ridiculous. The other cowboys were just being friendly.

Soon, Sadie went back to her chair and the roping started up again. He never lost his awareness of her, though. Ryder turned the lights on in the arena, and Knox could see her under the tree. Her voice carried over the fence as she called out encouragement, and everyone loved her applause at their efforts.

After they'd roped the last pen and the other guys had driven home, Sadie rode with him to turn the calves out. It was late, as usual, and they were quiet on the way back to the house.

Sadie settled back in her seat and sighed. "I had fun tonight."

"It's great having an audience. We're not used to it." He glanced over. Her white clothing gleamed in the darkness, and he glimpsed her gorgeous legs by the lights on the dash.

She yawned. "This Texas life makes me sleepy. Somehow it relaxes me, no matter what I'm doing."

His thoughts flashed to her in bed, naked and snuggled under one of his mom's homemade quilts, and he jerked them away. "I hope you sleep well tonight."

She looked over at him and smiled. "I'm sure I will. I feel amazing."

Back at the house, they headed to their rooms.

She stopped as she opened her door. "Good night, cowboy. I'll see you in the morning."

Her face was so happy, so sweet. His heart melted. "Good night, Sadie. Sleep well."

She grinned and shut the door behind her.

After a quick shower, he lay in bed, his thoughts returning to Sadie time and time again. Memories of their time together flooded him, and he wondered what it would be like to make love to her. And he ached, too, because that might never happen. Sadie would be crazy not to return to a job that paid in the millions. To consider that she would do anything else was plain nonsense.

Chapter Nine

Knox put on his hat and took a last look in the mirror. He stared at his face, at his shoulders and chest. What in the hell did New York guys look like? Were they more handsome than he was? Smoother? Surely they were more sophisticated. He frowned. To hell with them. He was a cowboy and damned proud of it.

He strode from his room and headed for the front of the house, surprised to find Sadie waiting in the living room. She was dressed in her Wranglers and boots, but damn, that blouse she was wearing. He refrained from giving a low whistle. The sexy gold shirt bared her shoulders and a bit of her belly. She was mouth-watering. He grinned. "I believe you're the prettiest cowgirl I've ever seen."

She grinned. "Thank you. I remembered you said not to dress up."

"I did. We're going to Stanton tonight to a little place called EJ's Cotton Pickin' Dive, and it has some of the best country cooking you'll find anywhere."

She laughed. "I love that name."

On the drive over, Sadie talked about their day together out on the ranch, her eyes sparkling with joy. After a lull in their conversation, she reached over and took his hand. Tingles shot through him at her touch, and he turned to look at her.

She smiled. "I like you, Knox. You're a good man."

"Thanks. I like you too, Sadie." She continued to stare at him, her gaze full of warmth, and he smiled back at her as excitement flooded his system. "It's been nice spending time with you."

She increased the pressure on his fingers. "You've made my time here really special. I don't know how to thank you."

He shrugged. "No need for that. I'm glad to have you around." He grinned. "Ranch work's never been this fun."

She chuckled. "Okay, then."

But she didn't let go of his hand. The connection sent heat flooding through his body. She held onto him until they pulled up to EJ's, and when she let go, he felt instantly colder.

He got her door and took her hand as she slid down from his truck. "I hope you find something vegetarian on the menu." He hadn't thought about that when he'd chosen their destination for the evening. He just wasn't used to thinking about that sort of thing. What an idiot.

She shrugged. "It won't be a problem. I'm used to making do. Don't worry."

As he escorted her inside, he placed his hand at her back. The soft, sensual texture of her bare skin at the hem of her blouse sent his heart racing.

When they walked through the door, the place was crowded, but there was one small table for two available. As they walked toward it, he noted that the men in the room couldn't take their eyes off his date. He grinned. They'd sure never seen anything like Sadie. Her long, dark-as-night hair hung in curls well below her shoulders, and the skin that showed at the bottom of her shirt—well, let's just say that the word "sexy" didn't cover it.

Sadie seemed oblivious to the attention as she looked over her menu. The small table hardly separated them, and he could sense her body from where he sat. His own body was tuned to her like a fine musical instrument.

She looked up. "I know what I'll order. How about you?"

"Sure do. They have the best chicken-fried steaks this side of the Colorado River." He closed his menu.

She smiled and leaned back in her chair, raising her voice to be heard over the buzz of conversation in the room. "This dinner's going to be epic."

He laughed. Epic? What the hell was she going to order? "Well, it's about time you let your hair down."

She grinned. "I'm finding myself relaxing a lot of rules these days, cowboy."

He raised his eyebrows. "You are?"

She nodded, her eyes full of mischief. "Sure am."

He let his eyes answer that, and she smiled.

They ordered dinner and talked about the ranch and what he had to do the following week until their food arrived.

She chuckled as the waitress slid her meal in front of her. "Now that's what I'm talking about!" Her plate was piled with biscuits literally smothered in white peppered gravy, and next to that nestled three eggs over medium. "I don't know how I'm going to eat all this, but I'm going to give it my best shot."

He grinned. "Go for it."

His chicken-fried steak, mashed potatoes and gravy, and corn came on a large platter, and he dug in, his mouth watering before he took his first bite. Damn, he loved this place.

As they talked during dinner, he sensed her attraction growing in the tilt of her head, in her smile, and in the sparkle in her eyes. His body responded. By the time they'd finished eating, he was on fire.

Taking a chance, he put his arm around her on the way out to the truck. She leaned her head against him, and a rush of desire swept through him.

On the drive home, she reached for his hand again, smiling at him with that spark in her eyes. He grinned and squeezed her fingers. She kept glancing at him on the thirty-minute drive home, as if to gauge his feelings for her. She needn't doubt him. Couldn't she sense his attraction?

He pulled up in front of the house and got out to open her door. When she slid down from the truck, instead of moving aside, he held her gaze. "Thanks for coming to dinner, Sadie."

She gave him a slow smile, then took his face in her hands and drew him close. Her lips brushed his, so softly he almost missed it. Then she kissed him harder, caressing every part of his mouth. She pressed kisses along his jaw and whispered in his ear, "I've wanted to kiss you for so long."

With a moan, he drew her into his arms.

She pulled back and met his gaze. "Kiss me, Knox. Like you mean it." He covered her mouth with a scorching kiss, exploring her, twining his tongue with hers. She whimpered and sucked his bottom lip. He cupped her head in his palms and angled his lips, delving deeper, claiming her as his own. She wrapped her leg around him and ran her fingers through his hair. He drew back, his brain buzzing with desire, but knowing that he needed to put on the brakes.

She smiled up at him and set her foot back on the ground. "I had fun tonight, Knox. Thanks for the great food." She grinned. "And for everything else."

She turned for the house, but he stayed put. He needed to calm his racing heart. To get his body under control. The last thing he'd wanted to do was stop. But he needed to be with Sadie when she'd had time to think it through. When she was sure what she was getting into. This wasn't that time.

He brushed his fingertips across his lips. Damn, she was gorgeous—and one hell of a good kisser. He smiled as the door closed behind her. *New York, you sleep good tonight, because I sure won't. I'll be awake thinking of you.*

SUNDAY MORNING, SADIE took a deep breath and told herself to relax. Just because they weren't riding in the arena, it didn't mean that she was in danger. She reached out and patted Sally's neck, more to reassure herself than anything.

She'd been surprised when she'd walked into the barn and had seen that Knox had saddled Sally with the beautiful, intricately carved trophy saddle from the tack room. When she'd asked why, he'd said, "Someone should use it, and it suits you. From now on, that's what we'll put on Sally when you ride." She had to admit, the padded seat was incredibly comfortable.

Knox glanced at her. "How're you holding up?"

"Fine. So, where are we going, exactly?"

He shrugged. "Nowhere in particular. We're just riding. The land looks different from horseback, don't you think?"

She looked around, something she hadn't done much of yet. She'd been a little too preoccupied with being nervous.

They were in a mesquite pasture, one that hadn't been cleared much. "What's that cactus called?" She pointed to a patch of rounded clumps with vicious-looking spiky thorns all over it.

"That's prickly pear cactus. When I clear a pasture, it's one of the first things I get rid of."

A little way farther on, it looked like something had turned over a large patch of earth. She pointed. "What caused that?"

Knox scowled. "Some damned wild hogs. They root around and tear up the land. Ruin good forage. They're a real pestilence."

The morning sun, warm at first, now felt hot. She was suddenly glad of the hat and the long-sleeved shirt she'd bought at the Western store. No wonder cowboys wore them.

Knox reached out from his saddle and clasped her hand. Her heart thumped, and she met his gaze. He smiled and squeezed her fingers. "Having fun?"

"I love it. This is such a beautiful place. It's so peaceful here. So quiet. I'd never noticed how noisy my life was until I came here and experienced a day with you."

"I like the quiet, too. Some people might think working alone all day would be lonely, but it's usually not like that for me. I feel..." He paused and looked all around him. "There's always something going on. I see deer, hawks, or a damn hog. There are jackrabbits, cottontails, lizards—we have some beautiful ones here. Something's always moving or making a sound. It's hard to feel alone."

She squeezed his fingers. "You have a wonderful life, Knox. I envy you."

He nodded. "I think so. This ranch has been in our family for four generations. I feel responsible for making it prosper.

That's a challenge with the drought that seems to have been going on forever and the low price of beef right now. I learned some stuff in college that I think can help. We need to change up the way we do things around here if the ranch is going to make it through my generation. The thought of it not doing that really worries me."

A wrinkle creased his brow as he looked off into the distance, lost in thought. He was an amazing man—good, honest, hardworking, and a wonderful son.

He turned back to her. "My grandparents moved into Abilene years ago when my father took over the ranch. They wanted to live close to a grocery store and the hospital, and my granny wanted a fenced-in yard for their old dog."

"I'll bet you miss them."

"I drop by when I can while I'm in town. I think grandpa misses the ranch. He comes out and visits sometimes. Likes to make sure we're doing things right." He chuckled.

She loved the way holding his hand felt—how it engulfed hers, making her feel so feminine and secure. She was completely relaxed now, not worried at all about falling off Sally or being outside the confines of the arena. Knox always made her feel safe, no matter where she was or what they were doing.

Knox had them following a pasture road that wended its way through the low rises and shallow dips in the wild landscape. Except for the road, it could have been a scene from the Wild West. He pointed to a dramatic plateau in the not-so-far distance. "That's also part of the ranch."

"It's beautiful. There're so many colors in this land. Not like the painted desert—I don't mean that. Just in the soil; the tans and oranges. It's wonderful."

Knox looked at her intently, as if he was surprised that she got it. "I think so too. Some people just see a desolate landscape, but it's so much more."

They continued their journey, occasionally opening a gate, and, by the time her butt and legs were crying out for respite, Knox called a halt at a copse of mesquite trees. "Let's take a break."

She groaned. "Thank God."

He chuckled. "We need to drink something, too. This heat will dehydrate us fast." He urged his horse ahead of hers and dismounted. "Stay on your horse for a minute. Let me help you down."

After tying his gelding to a limb, he walked over and clasped her calf. "Okay, swing your leg over and step down. Be careful. You might be a little wobbly."

Holding onto the saddle horn, she did as he'd told her, but when her foot hit the ground her leg buckled. "Oh!"

Knox grabbed her around the waist. "Steady!" He held onto her, supporting her weight, as she slipped her other foot out of the stirrup. Despite the weakness in her legs, her body tingled at the feeling of his hands on her.

After a moment, Knox released her with a smile. "Walk it off now. Get the blood flowing in those legs."

She grinned. "Not exactly the dismount I was aiming for."

He chuckled. "It happens to most people on their first long ride. Your legs will get used to it."

A few minutes later, she joined him where he sat in the shade under a tree.

He handed her a bottle of water he'd retrieved from one of the saddlebags. "Drink it all. You need it."

"You don't have to tell me twice. I'm thirsty." She sat close to him so that she could lean against the tree trunk as well. "This is nice. That sun is a beast." She hooked her arm through his, loving the feel of his body next to hers.

He moved, slipping his arm around her shoulders and pulling her against him. "Yeah, this is *real* nice." He grinned and took a swallow from his bottle. "You did good riding here today. You should be proud of yourself."

She leaned her head against him. "I was scared at first. All this wide-open space. I was worried that I'd lose control of Sally or that I'd fall off."

He squeezed her shoulders. "Nah. I wouldn't let that happen. Besides, Sally's a good horse. She'd never do anything tricky." He paused a moment, then said quietly, "You're going to get on a plane to New York one of these days. I'd sure like to kiss you again right now, but then that would be starting something between us and I don't know if that's right." He tilted her chin so that she met his gaze. "Sadie, you came here because you needed to heal. How is it going to help you if you go back to your life with a sore heart?"

She raised her hand to where he'd touched her face. "Let me worry about that. You make me feel good, Knox. Right here, right now, and I'm loving it." She let her eyes show him just how much she meant it.

He shook his head. "But what about later? What then? I want you to be happy, whole, and ready to be your old self when you step on that plane. Will you be able to do that?"

She sighed. God, he was sweet. She kissed his palm. "Knox, I'm not going to give up one hour, not one minute of being with you. But thank you for worrying about me." Smiling, she leaned close. "Now kiss me, and make it count."

A low growl rose from his throat and he kissed her, sweeping her lips in a passionate kiss that seemed to go on forever. She slid onto his lap and clasped his face in her hands, kissing him back, giving it everything she had. She wouldn't think about the future. She wanted, no *needed*, to be happy now. And that meant being with Knox McKinnis.

MONDAY MORNING, KNOX stepped into his boot and tugged it on. He couldn't bring himself to regret what had happened between himself and Sadie yesterday, but he did have some misgivings now that he'd had time to think about it. Although she'd told him in no uncertain terms not to worry about her, he still had a niggling worry that wouldn't let him alone.

Instead of heading to breakfast, he took a seat on his bed, heedless of the beautiful pieced quilt under him, and scrolled to Jessica's number in his phone. Her meetings shouldn't have started yet.

She answered on the second ring. "Good morning, big brother. How's it going?"

He smiled. She was such an upbeat person. It was one of the things he loved best about his baby sister. "Everything's good. I just wanted to talk to you for a couple of minutes. About Sadie."

"Really? Is something wrong?" She sounded worried.

"Oh, no. Not at all." Damn, he should have thought this through before he'd called her. "Listen, sis, you told me that

Sadie was having a hard time before she came here. Just how bad was it?"

She didn't answer right away. "What's this all about, Knox? Is something wrong with Sadie? Tell me!"

Dammit! He didn't want to tell Jessica about his feelings for her friend. Not yet, at least. "I'm telling you, she's fine." He took a deep breath. "Can you just tell me about her state of mind before she came to Texas...please?"

After a long moment, she said, "It was bad, Knox. Real bad. I won't betray a confidence, but she had me really worried. When she said that she wanted to come out here, I was so relieved. I knew it would do her a world of good. Knox, her life is something I wouldn't wish on anyone. It's so lonely. So cold. I don't know how she does it."

He clenched the phone. It was worse than he'd thought. "Thanks, sis. I appreciate you telling me. Listen, don't work too hard."

She chuckled. "I will. You know that."

He laughed. "Yes, I do. Bye, now."

He sat for a moment, considering the ramifications of the conversation with his sister. Despite her bravado, Sadie might be much more fragile than she was letting on. He had to put the brakes on.

During breakfast, he kept his gaze to himself, though he took part in the general conversation. Afterwards, Sadie followed him out to the truck. As they climbed in, he said, "We're heading over toward Abilene. I need a new heifer bull."

She buckled her seat belt. "That sounds interesting. What do you mean by a heifer bull? Is that something special?"

He backed the truck up to the stock trailer as he explained. "It's a bull that's genetically predisposed to throw small calves."

Before he got out to hitch the trailer to the truck, he said, "A heifer is a young female that hasn't had a calf before. Their pelvises are smaller, of course, so they have problems delivering big calves."

Soon they were on the road, and Sadie kept the conversation going. She seemed so happy. He almost couldn't bear the thought of never holding her in his arms again. He kept his right hand on the wheel just in case she tried to reach out and hold his hand. Though it was far from what his heart desired, he kept the conversation on ranching and off anything personal between them.

"So, is one reason that you're buying this bull to keep your bloodlines fresh?"

He looked at her, surprised that she'd sussed that out. "It sure is. You catch on pretty quick, New York."

She laughed. "I have my moments."

"Occasionally I'll keep a bull calf that has outstanding conformation for breeding, but then I have to be sure that I don't combine genetics in my herds." He took a turnoff. They were approaching the ranch that had the bulls for sale.

"It all sounds so complicated."

"It's just part of ranching. Not complicated. I have a book where I write bloodlines down. It helps me keep track of things."

They pulled down a long drive and parked in front of a barn where a pen held a number of bulls. They milled around, *maawing* in their general unhappiness at being with a bunch of other males.

Knox opened his door and turned to her. "You can get out." Even though she was dressed in a T-shirt and her Wranglers and boots, she looked stunning.

As the rancher came out of the barn, he took one look at her and his jaw dropped.

Knox smothered a smile as he walked over and offered his hand. "Jake, good to see you."

The man yanked his gaze away from Sadie and nodded at Knox. "Hey, Knox. Glad you stopped by. I've got some coming two-year olds caught up. I think you'll find something you like."

Sadie joined them and Knox said, "Jake, this is my sister's friend, Sadie Stewart. Sadie, this is Jake Fielding."

Sadie reached out her hand. "Nice to meet you."

Jake appeared tongue-tied for a few seconds, then said, "Likewise, Miss Stewart."

Sadie grinned. "Call me Sadie."

He nodded and headed for the old Chevy truck parked outside the barn. After removing some paperwork, he headed for the pen of bulls.

Knox followed him, Sadie at his side. Despite his intention of keeping his distance, his body was hyperaware of her, sensing her every move. Damn, this wasn't going to be easy. He walked to the gate, then glanced her way. "Stay out here, now. These young bulls are dangerous."

She nodded. "Okay. Be careful, huh?" She looked worried as he slipped inside.

Jake came in, too, and handed him several pages stapled together. "That's for #742. He's got some great stats."

Knox moved through the pen, looking at the ear tags on the different bulls until he spotted #742. He had decent conformation and moved well when he shooed him. Knox studied the bull's numbers. Not bad. The young males prowled around, and he had his hands full staying out of their way. It didn't pay to take your eyes off bulls this age.

Jake approached him again and handed him another sheaf of papers. Knox looked at the next bull. This was a well-muscled animal, right at two years old. He'd be a stout son of a gun. His stats looked good, too, and Knox liked his bloodlines.

When he'd examined all of the young bulls, he handed the paperwork back to Jake and pointed out the one he'd chosen. Jake nodded and called out, "Anson, come on over here!"

A couple of minutes later, a young man came walking over. "Knox here is taking #983. Let's load him up."

Knox glanced at Sadie. "Come on. We need to back the trailer up."

Moments later, the trailer was against the loading chute and Anson had separated the bull and had him heading down the alley toward the trailer. Knox stood ready to slam the middle door shut.

The young bull, excited at all of the commotion, came barreling down the alley. He slowed down at the narrow loading chute, but with the crack of Anson's stock whip above his back, he pushed his way through and jumped into the trailer. Knox slammed the gate and got back into the truck, pulling forward. Anson shut the back gate.

Knox glanced at Sadie as he climbed out again. "I'll just be a minute. I need to write Jake a check."

While he took care of that chore, his mind was on the beautiful woman back in the truck. He was having a hell of a time thinking about anything else today. He shook hands with Jake and returned to the truck.

Sadie smiled as he got in. "That was fun. You sure are brave. Those bulls were eyeing you like you were their next meal."

He laughed. "You have to stay on your toes around youngsters like that."

On the way home, he kept his hand on the wheel again. Sadie glanced at him often, as if sensing that something was different between them. He felt bad, but he'd feel a lot worse if she took a bad turn before she had to go back to New York.

When they got back to the ranch, he turned the young bull out with the heifers. He'd already removed the other bull and hauled him to the barn pasture.

Back at the house, they ate a late lunch.

After a few moments of silence, Sadie asked, "Is something wrong, Knox?"

He should have expected something like this—should have figured out something to say, dammit. "Um, Sadie, look..." He bit his cheek and avoided her gaze.

"What's going on, Knox?"

He sighed. "Look, when you leave, I want you to go back happy. I want you to have enjoyed every bit of your stay. That won't happen if you get hurt. Do you understand what I'm saying? I don't think it's a good idea for us to get involved."

Her face suddenly changed, and he realized that she was angry.

"So you think I'll fall head over heels in love with you, and then I'll have a broken heart?" she retorted. "Of all the conceited, arrogant men I've ever met, you've got to be the worst!" She shoved her chair back and rushed out of the room.

Stunned, he couldn't move. She was right. He was assuming that she'd fall for him. Did she mean that she was just into him for the physical thing? Why hadn't he thought of that? It hadn't felt like that to him when they were together, but he sure could have misread the whole deal. Damn, he was an idiot.

He picked up their plates and rinsed them in the sink. A few minutes later, as he headed out to feed at the north pasture, he realized that it just wasn't the same alone. He'd gotten used to having his cover girl riding shotgun.

Chapter Ten

Sadie flopped down on her bed, still shaking from her confrontation with Knox. Did the man think he was some kind of Galahad? She wasn't a helpless damsel in distress. She wanted the man, dammit! Why couldn't he just forget about everything else? She could tell that he wanted her too.

Her phone showed twelve-fifteen. Jessica should be at lunch, so she put in a quick call. "Hey, you busy?"

"Hi, Sadie. Just finishing lunch. How are you? How's everything going?" Sadie's friend sounded upbeat, as usual.

"Honestly? I'm ready to spit nails. That brother of yours..."

"Uh-oh. Tell me what happened."

Sadie sighed. "I've told you how attracted to him I am, right?"

Jessica chuckled. "Right."

"Well, the feeling's mutual. We've kissed a few times, and it's been wonderful. Then he just switched off. I couldn't figure it out, so I asked him about it. He said that it's just not going to work out between us. Apparently he thinks I'm too emotionally fragile or something."

Jessica was quiet a moment. "Sadie, he called me and asked about the reason you came to visit. He wanted to know just how bad things were for you before you came down here. I didn't share specifics, but I told him how serious it was. Honey,

I think that's why he's so worried. He cares about you, and he's trying to do the right thing."

He'd called Jessica? Asked about her past? Her first reaction was embarrassment. Then she realized that Jessica was right. Knox cared and was following his conscience. Warmth spread through her. He was such a wonderful man. She raised her hand to her lips as if she could take back the harsh words she'd said to him.

"Jessica, I think you're right. He's trying to be nice. I didn't understand. I owe him an apology. I'd better let you go. I can't wait until you get back here. I miss you!"

Her friend laughed. "I miss you too, Sadie. I won't be here too much longer. We'll have another girls' day and catch up on everything, okay?"

"You bet."

SADIE KEPT HER OWN counsel at dinner as Jeb and Knox talked about ranch business.

Maddie passed her more creamed corn. "Honey, I wish you'd get some meat on your bones."

Sadie smiled. "I sure don't need that, Maddie. I'm going back to work soon. I've purposely stayed off Jessica's scales while I've been here. I know I must have put on a few pounds with the way I've been eating."

Maddie shook her head. "Heck, you're just skin and bones, dear. A few pounds would do you good."

Sadie smiled. What a caring woman Maddie was. If only she'd had a mother like her, her life would have been so very different.

Knox glanced at her and smiled.

She sighed in relief. He'd forgiven her for her outburst. Thank goodness. She smiled back and took a bite of corn. Man, she loved the stuff. Maddie was a fabulous cook.

After dinner, she helped with the dishes, as she always did in the evenings, then felt restless. With nothing particular in mind, she headed out to the barn. After looking unsuccessfully for the barn cat, she walked over to lean on a post of the pasture fence and watched the horses grazing on the pale-green grass.

The evening sun, though low in the sky, still had some heat to it. She closed her eyes. A hoof stomped the ground, ridding one of the horses of flies. A dove called in the distance. She loved that sound. It was beautiful but melancholy. A bee buzzed at the wild onion flower she'd noticed at her feet when she'd walked up. Knox had been right. A person could never feel alone on this ranch.

She opened her eyes as Sally blew a loud, wet breath through her nose and shook her head. Flies again. They were the bane of a horse's existence.

She looked down at her sandaled feet, at her French-manicured toenails that looked so out of place on a Texas ranch, and realized that she wanted to fit in here. She wanted to be a part of this special place. Leaning her chin on the fence post, she let her eyes wander to the horizon, to the hazy green of the mesquite pasture in the distance and the deep oranges and golds of the evening sky. Beauty was everywhere, and peace lay over it like a soft mantle. She was happier here than she'd ever been in her life.

When the last curve of the orange sun disappeared, she turned and made her way back to the house. As she climbed the front porch steps, she found Knox on the old porch swing.

He smiled at her.

She joined him, her mind clear and calm. "Knox, I'm so sorry for the way I spoke to you today. I know you're trying to protect me. I spoke to Jessica, and she told me that you'd called her." She reached out and clasped his hand. "You've been so good to me. I should have realized that you had my best interests at heart."

He tightened his hold on her fingers. "Sadie, your happiness means everything to me. I can't stand the thought of you hurting again. I want to make sure that doesn't happen." He looked into her eyes, and she could see how much he cared.

"Knox, I feel so good now. This place has healed me. A few moments ago, I had the thought that I'm happier than I've ever been." She leaned toward him. "I'm stronger than I've ever been." Reaching up, she stroked his cheek. "Us, being together, it's okay. Please don't worry."

He gazed into her eyes for a moment, then nodded.

She smiled and pushed the swing into motion, settling against the wooden slats. He slipped his arm around her, and she nestled her head against him. Closing her eyes, she savored the feeling of his strong body wrapped around hers, the masculine smell of him, his hand caressing her arm. She didn't think often about heaven, but this must be what it was like.

Soon, though, the tiny biting evening gnats arrived—and they always found her particularly delicious. She scrubbed at her bare arms, then scratched her leg. "Damn these gnats. How come they never seem to bother you?"

He smiled. "I'm too bitter."

She rolled her eyes. "Does that mean I'm sweet?"

He squeezed her tight. "Maybe I'll find that out one of these days."

She laughed and stood up. "I'm going in. I can't stand being dinner for these bugs any longer."

He got up too. "Be ready at breakfast. We have a lot to do tomorrow."

Her heart soared. "No problem." As she walked inside, she could feel his eyes on her. What would it be like to have his hands all over her body instead? Maybe soon she'd find out.

THE NEXT MORNING, KNOX glanced over the back of his horse at Sadie as he looped the cinch onto the saddle. "Like I said at breakfast, we're heading out to the south pasture today to castrate calves and give them their shots. Then we'll deworm the whole herd." He pulled the cinch strap tight and tied it off at the D ring, then flopped the stirrup down. He'd wait and bridle the gelding when they got to the pasture, so he tied the bridle to his saddle horn with the latigo straps.

Sally was saddled and stood haltered and ready to go. His dad had already loaded his horse in the trailer.

Jeb came into the barn and untied Sally. "You ready to ride this morning, Sadie?" He smiled when he said it, obviously fond of her.

"Yes, sir."

"Now you hang back while we gather the herd. I don't want you getting hurt. Sally here's an old hand at roundup, and she might get it into her head to take off after a straggler that gets away from us."

"I'll do that, don't worry."

He nodded and led the horse out of the barn.

Knox caught her attention as he stepped away from his horse. "He's serious, now. You hold back. I considered having you stay home. Sally's no slouch. She's a gentle thing, but she knows her way around cattle, and I don't want her getting it in-to her head that she needs to help with the roundup."

Sadie nodded again. "I promise. I won't go near the herd. I don't want to fall off, believe me."

He grinned. "No, you don't. It hurts."

She laughed. "You're telling me you've fallen off a horse?"

"Sure, when I was a kid. I got pretty full of myself once and took a really hard fall. Broke my arm." He led his horse out to-ward the trailer, and Sadie walked beside him. It felt great hav-ing her along today. Their talk last night had cleared things up for him. He'd decided to trust Sadie's instincts about their rela-tionship.

The two border collies danced around beside the trailer. They always knew something fun was up when the horses were saddled and loaded. He led the gelding into the back of the trailer, then shut the gate.

Sadie rode in the middle of the truck's front seat, between him and his dad. His body buzzed as her shoulder brushed his. When they got to the pasture, Knox drove to the stock pond, hoping that the herd would be there. Judging by what he could see of the tracks near the water, however, they'd already been and gone.

He parked, and they got out and unloaded the horses. The herd probably wasn't far. He helped Sadie mount, thrilling at the feel of her calf beneath his fingers. She gathered the round rein in her hand and looked pretty confident. He patted her thigh. "You've got this. Remember, stay back once we find the cattle."

She nodded, her face calm. "Got it. Don't worry about me, Knox. Just do your thing."

He mounted and glanced at his father, whose horse was already walking down the road away from the water.

Knox looked at Sadie again. "Let's go. Keep up." Never having been cleared, the south pasture was wild with mesquite and full of cactus. They soon left the road. Sadie stayed right beside him. "Let Sally pick her way," he told her. "She'll avoid the prickly pear and other cactus on her own. You don't need to worry."

They found the herd fifteen minutes later. Knox stopped a good distance away and glanced at Sadie. "Hold up here. We'll get the herd moving. Don't start out until I call you."

She nodded. "I understand. I won't move."

"Keep tight hold of the reins. Don't relax. Sally'll be watching the cattle. You don't want her getting any ideas."

He studied Sadie's face. She seemed to understand the gravity of her situation. Sally should be all right unless a cow came right for her. Then the old girl would feel like she needed to do something about it. "If it looks like Sally's getting interested, just pull back on the reins and say, 'Whoa!' She'll mind."

"Okay. We'll be fine."

Sadie seemed a little nervous now. That was good too. It would keep her on her toes.

His dad had moved on around to the other side of the herd. The cattle had their heads up and were milling around. Knox rode in, and it didn't take long to get them moving in the direction of the catch pens. Those were a distance away, so it would take a while to get them there. The herd wasn't new to making a trip to the pens, though, so they didn't put up much of a fuss. He looked back over his shoulder as he called out, "Come on now," and waved his arm at Sadie.

She waved back and Sally moved ahead.

He smiled. Sadie looked so happy. And so very beautiful.

The easiest way to get to the pens was down the dirt road, so that's where they headed the herd. The cattle kept to a steady walk, knowing where they were going and that food waited for them in the troughs in the catch pen. His father had gone out early and made sure of that.

A couple of minutes later, he glanced back again. Sadie came steadily forward, looking confident in the saddle. Even better, her horse was calm, plodding along with no interest in the cattle ahead.

He relaxed. This was a wonderful experience for Sadie. She'd never forget getting to work cattle on a ranch in Texas. He planned on letting her help with castrating the calves. Remembering her composed reaction to the bull's abscess when she first arrived, he expected that she'd have the stomach for it.

They made it to the road, and the cattle easily turned onto it. Occasionally one cow or another would try to leave the herd and either he or his dad would have to run it back to the others.

Suddenly a crafty old cow broke from the stragglers and headed back towards Sally. Knox spurred his gelding, but he was on the other side of the herd and the cow slipped past him.

In horror, he watched helplessly as Sally's head came up and she launched herself at the oncoming cow.

Sadie cried out and reached for the saddle horn, careening sideways as Sally dove, attempting to cut the old cow off.

Knox was too far away to help as he yelled, "Hold on, Sadie!" He dug his heels into his gelding, his horse springing into a run.

Somehow, Sadie stayed in the saddle. Sally, like the good cowhorse she was, beat the old cow to the punch and headed her back toward the herd. As the old horse settled into a walk again, Sadie, looking scared to death, pulled herself straight again.

Knox arrived at her side and reached for her. "My God, are you okay?" He was shaking inside, his hands trembling as he held his excited gelding still.

She nodded, "I thought I was a goner."

He took off his hat and wiped his brow. "If you'd gotten hurt..." He couldn't bear to think about it.

"I'm fine. Now I'll have a great cowgirl story to tell."

He tried to grin, but it was a poor effort. Why in the hell had he let her come along today? "I want you to stay a lot farther back from now on, okay? I don't want Sally to get any more bright ideas."

She chuckled. "Not a problem."

The rest of the drive was uneventful, thank God.

As they neared the pens, he rode ahead and opened the gate. Then he moved out to the side to act as a buffer. There were always those cows who balked at entering the pen. He called out to Sadie, "Stop there. That's close enough."

Sure enough, two cows peeled from the herd, dodging away from the entrance. His gelding went after them, and they quickly turned back and entered the gate. The cattle eagerly lined up at the troughs, which were made out of metal barrels cut in half. He let them eat and settle down after the more-than-hour-long drive.

He shut the gate as Sadie rode up. "How you holding up?"

"This was fun. Sally's such a good horse." She leaned over and patted her neck.

"That she is."

Sadie's face glowed. There was such joy brimming from her eyes. The shadows that had been there when she'd first arrived were nowhere to be seen.

It took some work, but soon he and his dad had the calves separated from their mothers and into the pen with the small head gate.

While his dad worked at deworming the rest of the herd and giving the late-stage pregnant cows a 7-way shot, Knox ran several calves into the pen's little alley and shut the gate behind them.

Sadie was in the pen with him, standing nervously against the fence. He called her over to the head gate and clasped the lever. "You see this?"

She nodded.

"I'll run a calf into this chute, and he's going to shove his head through this gate. When he does, I want you to yank down on this lever, hard, and it'll pin his neck and hold him in." He pointed to a curved opening in the gate. "See this? It keeps the thing from choking the calves."

She nodded her understanding but looked apprehensive.

He smiled and patted her on the back. "Relax. It doesn't hurt them at all. You've got this. Now, put your hand on the lever and get ready while I tail that first calf."

He stepped to the back of the chute and yanked up on the calf's tail. The calf jumped forward into the chute, bursting into the head gate.

Sadie hauled on the lever, and it clanked shut with a bang, trapping the calf's neck.

He laughed. "Way to go!"

She grinned, obviously proud of herself.

He handed her the gallon jug of dewormer and the wand. "Now squirt this on his back while I remove his boy parts." He glanced up as he made the first cut and noticed Sadie's shocked expression.

"Don't you deaden it with anesthetic first?" She licked her lips as her face paled.

He should have thought of this. "No, it just takes a few seconds. You notice that he didn't even yell."

She frowned. "He kicked, though. I know he felt the knife."

He grimaced. He really should have realized that she'd feel sorry for the calf. This was a bad idea.

"Sadie, I'm sorry. I shouldn't have asked you to come along today. This is too upsetting for you."

She shook her head and let out a loud breath. "Just hurry. The poor thing is suffering. I just can't believe that this is how ranchers castrate their animals."

He quickly finished the job as Sadie squirted the wormer on the calf's back. He called, "Let him out!"

She released the gate and turned her back to him, her arms folded across her chest.

He stepped out of the alley and put his hand on her shoulder. "Look, we could have the vet castrate the calves, but it's expensive. And time-consuming. A vet would inject the testicles with an anesthetic and then wait for it to take effect. Then he'd open up the ball sack, pull out the testicle, clamp the cord, and wait five minutes before he cut it. After that, he'd repeat the process on the second testicle."

She turned to look at him.

"Imagine the cost and the time it would take with twenty to twenty-five calves to run through. We don't have that kind of money or time. There's just two of us running this operation. We run ourselves ragged trying to keep up with things around here. How we castrate is the way it's been done for ages." He pointed at the calf that had just been released from the chute. "He's walking just fine. There's only a tiny bit of blood on his hind end. He'll forget all about what happened by feeding time tonight."

She stared at the young animal for a moment. "I guess I just wasn't prepared for what happened."

"That's my fault. I should have explained it and given you a chance to stay home."

She shook her head and scuffed her shoe in the dirt. "No, I'm glad I came. I wanted to learn about ranching, and this is part of it."

She stepped up to the chute. "Let's get this show on the road."

He nodded. She was something else, all right.

As they ran calf after calf through the chute, he enjoyed having her working beside him. It filled a need that he'd never experienced before. He and his father were a good working team, but this was something different. This was like...like he'd found a soulmate.

Many of the calves were heifers, so they only squirted them with dewormer and ran them out of the chute. It was a dusty, dirty job, and he admired Sadie's work ethic. She didn't even seem to mind the occasional splat of manure that came through the bars of the chute.

A couple of hours later, the last cow ran through the big head gate. Knox opened the pen and the cattle filed out into the pasture.

It didn't take long for Maddie to arrive to pick them up. Knox sat in the back with Sadie. He reached over and patted her knee. "You did a great job today. You should be proud of yourself."

She grinned. "Despite nearly falling off my horse, I had a blast. Thanks for letting me ride along."

He gave her a leg squeeze. "I enjoyed having you alongside me. You were a big help. It would have taken a lot longer to get through the herd if you weren't with us today."

"Really?" She grinned, happiness oozing from every pore.

"Truly. Normally, Dad and I have to work together. Today, we had two chutes going. We got done in half the time."

"Wow!" Sadie's smile lit up her face. She looked like a kid with a pile of Christmas presents.

When they got to the truck and trailer, Jeb looked back at them. "You all go on to the house. I'll see to the horses."

Knox frowned. "You sure?"

"Yep. Sadie did the work of two men today." He grinned at her. "You're a good hand, honey. Thanks for your help."

Knox didn't think she could look happier, but it happened. She literally shone with joy.

"Thank you, Jeb. I appreciate you and Knox including me."

When they arrived back at the house, he glanced at Sadie. "I need to check the heifers in the barn."

"I'll come with you."

His pulse picked up speed as she strode beside him, his body aware of her every move.

In the barn, Sadie stood close as he leaned on one of the pens, eyeing the heifer pacing inside. The ground showed several places where she'd been lying down. She was near her time and, by her anxious behavior, probably feeling contractions. "It won't be long for this young girl. I'll need to check on her again in a little while."

"How do you know?"

Her voice, so low and sexy, had its usual effect on him, and he wanted to take her in his arms. Working beside her all day had done something to him; brought a new realization of how much he cared about her. Her eyes, like the darkest chocolate, showed her emotions so easily. He explained the signs he'd seen, his body humming with attraction all the while.

She placed her hand on his arm. "Knox?" She had the tiniest of smiles on her lips.

"Hmm?"

"I want to kiss you."

His heart leapt, and he pulled her into his arms, crushing her to his chest. "You're sure?"

She nodded.

He cupped her face in his hands and looked into her eyes, reading nothing but joy there. He kissed her then, gently, taking his time, letting her feel how he cherished her.

She slid her hands up his arms and wrapped her arms around his neck. She kissed him back with an urgency that spoke of her need.

He pulled her close, his body hard, responding to that need. He wanted her. Wanted to get to know this beautiful, strong woman who had overcome such a tragic past.

She raked her hands through his hair and kissed him hard. He moaned and gave as good as he got, forgetting about his misgivings. She was his now.

He wasn't sure how long they explored each other, but finally he drew her arms from his neck and stepped away. Her eyes were glazed with passion—as he was sure his own were. He drew a deep breath and smiled. "We're in it now, cover girl."

She grinned. "Indeed we are, cowboy."

He took her by the hand and headed for the open doors. There was no going back now.

Chapter Eleven

That night, Sadie lay in bed, her mind swirling with memories of Knox. His eyes as he looked at her. The kindness in them. The goodness. How his arms felt when he held her. How his strong hand felt when he touched her. She was so thankful he'd finally accepted that she wasn't some fragile thing that would break at the slightest touch.

She wanted more than what they'd already shared. She wanted to give the deepest part of herself to him. She knew he was safe.

And she wanted to reach deep inside him. To touch that core that made Knox the incredible man he was. She wanted all of him.

Tossing the covers aside, she adjusted her short negligée and crept to the door. It opened quietly, and she tiptoed down the hall and silently opened Knox's door. Shadows filled the room, but with the moonlight coming in the window, she could see him in the bed.

He raised up. "Sadie?"

She stepped through and eased the door shut behind her. "Yes," she whispered.

Knox stood from the bed, clothed only in a pair of dark briefs.

She moved to him, and he reached for her. "Something wrong?"

Slipping her arms around his neck, she met his gaze in the dim light.

His hands found her waist. "You sure about this?"

He smelled wonderful, sending her heart speeding even faster, and she put her lips to his ear. "More than anything in my life."

His arms slid around her, and he let out a sigh. "You feel good."

She traced the shell of his ear with the tip of her tongue, and he drew in a sharp breath.

His arms tightened. "Sadie." He kissed her temple. "I'm glad you're here." Then he picked her up and laid her in the middle of the bed. Gazing down on her, he brushed his knuckles across her cheekbone. "I've dreamed about you lying here just like this." He brushed a soft kiss across her lips. "You're beautiful. So very, very beautiful. But you know what I love even more about you?"

She shook her head, too overwhelmed at being with him, at having his body so close to hers. Without thought, she reached for him.

He kissed her again. "I love how sweet you are. You're such a good person, Sadie."

She could only whisper, "Thank you." Her hands had a mind of their own, molding themselves to the hard outlines of his muscular chest.

He smiled down on her, his hand lifting the hem of her short negligée.

She whispered, "Take it off."

"With pleasure."

As she raised herself slightly, he quickly slipped it over her head, then gusted out a breath. "My God, you're gorgeous." He ran his fingers lightly across the curve of her waist. "I'm a lucky man."

She smiled. "Your turn."

He chuckled. "Right." His briefs were off in a heartbeat. He slid his leg over hers, and her pulse quickened. His broad body made her feel so small despite her length.

She slipped her hand behind his neck, feeling the taut tendons there, and drew him down to her lips. A gentle kiss drew a soft sigh from him. Running a hand up his hard, muscled back, she claimed his lips in a slow, sensual kiss that lasted for several breaths. When he drew back, his face was soft, filled with a sweet caring that matched her own.

His hand slid across her belly and cupped her breast. She relished the intimacy of it, the sense of being one with him. He rubbed his thumb across her taut nipple, sending a shockwave of pleasure through her. She smiled and he bent, taking it in his mouth, and she gasped at the incredible sensations his tongue created. Every part of her was intensely alive to his touch.

She cradled his head in her hands and closed her eyes, giving in to the waves of sensation he created. She sighed when he moved to her other breast, her pleasure heightening even more.

His hand slid down her hip to her panties and tugged. She rose up, and he quickly slid them off. Excitement filled her as she anticipated what he might do next. He paused to kiss her, and she kissed him back, hard, her passion rising with each passing second.

He grinned and kissed her belly, once, twice, then again at her soft curls. She sucked in a breath as he paused there. His fingers traced a line down her thigh, tickling her. She ran her fingers through his hair, tingles racing through her, the anticipation more than she could bear.

He kissed her thigh and she jerked, too sensitive to his touch. He laughed and moved between her legs. Her heart hammered. Her core clenched. He cupped her butt in his strong hands and slipped his tongue inside her. She nearly cried out with the ecstasy of it. Clenching the sheets in her fists, she lost all coherent thought as he found her sensitive spot, caressing it, stroking it. Involuntary tremors of arousal began. Heat scorched through her. Her head tossed from side to side at the intensity of sensation as his tongue worked relentlessly. She breathed in deep, soul-drenching drafts.

She lost all track of time, floating in a world of incredible sensation. Suddenly she shattered as waves of ecstasy throbbed through her. "Knox!" She pulled at his shoulders.

He rose above her and reached into the bedside table, slipping on a condom as she whimpered her need. He kissed her quickly, then eased himself inside her. She gasped as he filled her completely. God, he felt so good. He pulled out and thrust harder. She gripped him, wanting him deep inside. She was still pulsing as pleasure washed through her in waves.

Knox thrust hard, reaching his rhythm. She opened her eyes. Watching his deepening excitement

only increased her own. She closed her eyes again, lost in the incredible experience her lover created. She floated on waves of bliss, her soul connected as one with Knox's. With a last thrust, he gasped and threw back his head, his body frozen as she felt him pulse inside her. She clasped his arms, her own pleasure still resonating.

A moment later, Knox kissed her gently and rolled on his side, pulling her over to spoon against his chest. "You were wonderful, Sadie."

She chuckled and ran her hand up his arm. "No way, you're the one who was wonderful." She turned over to face him and kissed him gently. He looked into her eyes and smiled, and her heart melted.

Brushing her hair back from her face, he whispered, "I'm glad." Then he brought her fingers to his lips. "Will you stay with me tonight?"

She smiled. "I'd love to. Fair warning, though. I'm a restless sleeper."

"Maybe I can do something about that. Turn over now. Let me hold you."

When he had her cuddled safely in his arms again, he whispered in her ear, "Good night, cover girl. I'm so glad you're here."

WEDNESDAY MORNING, before dawn, he woke to find that Sadie had already gone. After dressing, he went down to the kitchen and made coffee, too keyed up to go back to sleep. Making love to Sadie had been incredible. He could still feel her, taste her kisses. He'd remember last night forever.

He went out on the porch to the swing. The sun, still below the horizon, lit the sky with an early pale light. He set the swing in motion and let his mind roam. Emotions swirled inside him as memories of Sadie flickered past. Somehow, she'd become the center of his world.

Steam rose from his mug and he took a tentative sip. A horse blew noisily from its nostrils. A heifer *maawed* from the barn pens. A mourning dove gave its plaintive call in the distance. A cool breeze picked up, brushing across his face. The ranch was waking from the still silence of night.

He couldn't imagine living somewhere that he couldn't experience these simple things. The sights and sounds were woven into his being.

Poor Sadie. He could only imagine the awfulness that she awakened to each morning. Cars honking, ambulance sirens wailing, brakes squealing. No animals. No birds. It was no wonder that she felt happy here.

He took another scalding sip. He didn't want her to go back. *There. I've admitted it.* It was an impossible wish, but he wanted her to stay here, in Texas, with him. He accepted it for what it was—a selfish want. Sadie's life was back east. Her multi-million-dollar job, her home, everything. But he couldn't stand the thought of losing her.

The screen door creaked in its usual needing-to-be-oiled way, and Sadie walked out. "You're up early, cowboy."

"So are you, New York." He smiled as she joined him on the swing, holding a cup of coffee that steamed in the cool morning air. The sun peeked above the horizon, sending streaks of gold, soft pink, and orange across the sky.

She sighed, her gaze wandering over the landscape. "It's so beautiful here."

"It is." He reached for her free hand and twined his fingers with hers, feeling a wonderful new sense of peace and contentment. Shoving off with his feet, he set the swing in motion.

She leaned back and squeezed his hand. "I seldom see this part of the day. It's wonderful. Just look at that sunrise."

"So you sleep in?"

She smiled. "I guess I should rephrase that. I get up early to catch my flights a lot. Then I see buildings all around me except for the park below my windows. A beautiful sunrise like this? No way."

"I'd hate that."

She took a sip from her mug. "Now that I've experienced this place, I'll despise it." She frowned. "I hate thinking about how little time I have left here. The spring season show is getting nearer and nearer." She patted her belly. "I hope I fit in the clothes. I wonder how much weight I've put on?"

He chuckled. "I don't think you've put on any. You look fabulous."

She smiled. "I've been eating like a pig. I know I have. I just don't want to know how much. Not yet." She picked at the seam in her jeans. "I can lose it pretty fast. If I go back a little early, I'll be okay."

His heart fell. *Go back early? No. She couldn't.*

After breakfast, they helped Jeb load up the horses and headed out to the steer pasture. They had a busy day ahead of them. The market price was good right now, and they were going to sell the ones that were ready.

After his dad unloaded the horses, and before Knox could help Sadie mount, she stepped into the stirrup and rose to the saddle herself. He grinned. "Nice job. You're getting the hang of this cowgirl thing."

It took them a while to reach the herd, and he enjoyed having her riding close beside him.

"This is such beautiful country." It was the first thing she'd said in a while.

"I sure think so." Yes, the place they were riding was beautiful, but Sadie was gorgeous. He couldn't keep his eyes off her, and every few minutes he thought about the fact that she would be leaving soon. It was hard keeping his mind on the business of the day.

They found the herd about where he'd expected them to be. Sadie hung back while he and Jeb got them in motion. The dogs were a lot of help. Once they had them headed in the right direction, Sadie followed behind on Sally.

When they arrived at the pens and got the cattle inside, they all dismounted and tied the horses to the fence. Knox gave Sadie a stock whip. "We need to run the larger ones into that smaller pen. We'll load them up from there."

She nodded.

He was amazed at how unafraid she was as they worked among the herd. Cattle were big animals, and Sadie could easily have been hurt if she hadn't stayed on her toes. She kept one eye on him, awaiting directions, and the other on the milling herd. It was dusty, hard work separating the biggest steers from the others. Jeb let the two of them handle the job, only occasionally calling out instructions to Sadie.

Eventually, the job was done. Knox checked the group of steers one more time, just to be sure he hadn't made a mistake and included one too small, then called out, "Sadie, turn 'em out."

"Got it." She opened the big gate, and the rest of the steers filed out into the pasture.

Meanwhile, Jeb had called Maddie. She'd arrive in a few minutes to take him to get the truck and trailer.

Knox walked over to Sadie and slapped her on the back. "Great job today, cowgirl. You were a big help."

She grinned. "That was fun. I'm kind of tired, though. Those steers can move fast."

He chuckled. "But you did good. I'm impressed." He admired how she'd never complained, not once since she'd started working with him.

She met his gaze, and the joy in her eyes was wonderful to see. She was such a different person from the snooty Easterner he'd met that first night. She was going to be sore this afternoon after riding and then working the cattle so hard in the pen.

They got back mid-afternoon, way past lunchtime. Maddie fixed them sandwiches.

Sadie ate quickly, then got up and rinsed her plate. "God, I need a shower. I'm half dust right now."

Knox laughed. "I do think you look a little tan."

Her eyes widened and she glanced at her hands, which had been gloved, then raised them to her cheeks.

"I'm just kidding. You don't, silly. Go clean up."

She rolled her eyes. "If I get a farmer tan, I'm in serious trouble for the show. My sunscreen had better work."

He shook his head, but her comment sent a pang to his chest, reminding him that he'd lose her soon.

He finished eating and headed up to shower too. The only other thing he had planned for the day was feeding at the barn.

He ended up taking a nap, something totally out of character for him. But he'd lain down to close his eyes for a few minutes and had drifted off to sleep.

When he walked into the kitchen, Sadie was helping his mom with dinner. She smiled at him. "Hey, sleepyhead. Dinner's almost ready."

She looked good enough to eat in a pair of shorts and a T-shirt that showed off her sexy figure perfectly. Though they'd eaten a late lunch, he was hungry. "Smells good."

"Your mom's teaching me how to cook. I might be pretty good at it by the time I leave here. I've even figured out how to adapt several of the recipes to my vegetarian needs."

His heart panged again, and he sighed. Then he realized that he needed to say something. "You're learning from the best."

She grinned. "I know I am." She put her arm around Maddie and gave her a squeeze. "You're lucky to have such a talented mom."

Maddie chuckled. "Oh, go on with you, now. I learned everything from my mother. I don't use cookbooks or anything."

"You don't need them. You could write your own cookbook." Sadie got out the plates and set the table. After putting out the silverware, she added a glass to each place.

Knox's heart warmed at this sweet, domestic scene. What would it be like to have Sadie here every night? He'd give anything to find out. With a sigh, he headed out to the barn to feed.

Sadie and Maddie talked about family recipes during dinner, while he and his father made plans for the following day. He kept glancing across the table and listening to the sound of Sadie's low, slightly husky voice. Did she have any idea how sexy she sounded?

After dinner, he headed out to the porch swing. He'd offered to help clean up, but his mom had shooed him from the room.

Soon, Sadie joined him. She leaned back and sighed.

"Tired?" He reached for her hand.

"Oh, yeah. Worn out. I'm using muscles here I never knew I had, and they're yelling at me about it."

He could do something about that. "Lean forward."

She turned to him, her eyebrows raised.

"Go on, do it and turn away from me."

He began to massage her shoulders.

She let out a long sigh. "That's marvelous, Knox. Don't stop."

He chuckled. Careful not to squeeze too hard, he paid attention to her slender neck as well. She felt incredible under his fingers. He loved touching her.

Her head lolled and he smiled, wanting to take her in his arms. Memories from the previous night flooded his mind.

At last, she straightened. "Thank you, Knox. I feel amazing, and I can barely keep my eyes open. I'm going to bed." She turned and kissed his cheek, her gaze warm and happy.

She groaned when she stood up, and he laughed. "We have another long day tomorrow. You sure you're up to it?"

"Don't even think of leaving me at home, cowboy."

He decided to head to bed, too, but lay awake when he got there, reliving making love to the beautiful woman in the room next door. He'd been so worried about how badly Sadie might feel when she returned to New York that he truly hadn't considered what would happen to him. He had such strong feelings for her now. His heart thumped. He might even be falling in love with her.

How could he bear to see her go? To never see her again? The answer was, he couldn't. An ache started deep inside him, and he didn't figure it was going away anytime soon.

Chapter Twelve

I*s it too much?* Sadie turned so that she could see herself from behind in the full-length mirror in Jessica's room. She was dressed in a baby-blue sateen strapless bustier and matching high-waisted, pencil-legged pants that she'd unzipped at the bottom so that they hung over her four-inch heels. She'd be nearly as tall as Knox tonight. Her dark hair was pulled into a ponytail at the top of her head and hung down her back. She wore no jewelry save for diamond studs in her ears.

Knox had invited her to go country-and-western dancing with him and his friends tonight, but she hadn't been able to bear the idea of dressing in her jeans and boots—not after wearing them in cow poop for days.

Besides, she loved this outfit. Satisfied with her appearance, she tucked a lipstick in her pocket and headed for the living room.

Knox's eyes widened when she entered, and he gave her a slow smile.

She turned in a circle. "Too much?"

After a low whistle, he said, "Sure as hell not for me. You're gorgeous."

She laughed. "Thanks, cowboy."

"You look pretty, honey," Maddie said from her seat on the couch.

"Thank you. I love this color."

Knox took her hand. "I just heard from Blake. They've already headed out, so we need to get a move on."

When they got out onto the main highway, she reached for Knox's hand.

He turned to her and grinned. His eyes gleamed in the evening light. He seemed excited tonight.

She said, "I never told you this, but your mom had a talk with me a while back. She wants me to be careful with you."

He drew his brows together. "Seriously? That surprises me."

She nodded. "It surprised *me*, but I realized that she was just worried about you. She knows that I have to go back to my world at some point." Her heart fell at saying the words out loud.

"I don't want to think about that, Sadie," Knox said quietly.

"Me neither."

He squeezed her hand, his face suddenly solemn.

They drove in silence for a while, and the connection she experienced through their clasped hands comforted her.

They arrived at the Bee Hive restaurant, and Knox pointed out Blake's truck. "This place is known for its excellent beef. Too bad you don't eat meat."

"I'm sure I'll find something I'll enjoy. Being vegetarian isn't so awful, you know."

He grinned. "It would be for me. I like my steaks."

She smiled and shook her head as he helped her down from the truck.

When they got inside, Knox spotted Blake right away. He leaned toward Sadie and said, "His date's name is Allison. She's new. I've never met her before."

Once they were seated, Blake made introductions.

Sadie noticed Allison taking in her outfit with an interested look. She was dressed more conservatively than Sadie, but she was a pretty blonde and had a nice smile.

"Do you live on a ranch, Allison?" Sadie asked her.

"Oh, no. I live in Abilene. That's where Blake and I met. Do you?"

"I'm staying with Knox's sister, Jessica, right now, but I live in New York City."

Allison's eyes widened. "That's so amazing. What's it like?"

"Compared to the ranch?" Sadie thought for a moment. "Busy, noisy, crowded. I'll miss all of the colors here when I go back."

Knox reached for her hand.

She met his gaze, and his eyes were as troubled as she knew hers were.

After a pleasant dinner, they headed for the dance hall. She and Knox clung to each other's hands as he drove. She wanted to cherish every moment with him, and he seemed to feel the same way.

When they entered, the place was already crowded and the band was on a break. Knox took her by the hand as he gazed around the smoke-filled room.

"Over there." Blake pointed to the far side of the room and headed in that direction.

They walked quickly to make sure that nobody took the empty table before they could claim it for themselves. Sadie, in her four-inch heels, barely managed to keep up.

Knox finally noticed and slowed. "Sorry about that."

She grimaced. "These shoes might have been a poor choice for the evening."

He grinned and put his arm around her waist. "No way. You look hot."

She laughed and put her arm around him too, clasping his belt. "You look incredibly handsome yourself tonight."

When they got to the table, Knox held her chair. "First round's on me if you'll help me carry it, Blake."

His friend grinned. "Let's go."

As the guys headed for the bar, Allison leaned forward. "It's a Red Dirt band tonight. I love that music."

Sadie raised her brows.

"Oh, Red Dirt has a great beat. It's fast and rowdy and amazing to dance to," Allison explained.

"Sounds great." The dance hall was packed with crowded tables, and other customers hung out at the railing surrounding the dance floor. There were three bars in the building, all of which were three-deep in people waiting to order. Waitresses hurried between tables, delivering drinks. The place was definitely hopping tonight.

Eventually, the guys returned, and Knox set Sadie's wineglass in front of her. She smiled her thanks, and he sat down and slipped his arm around her shoulders. She leaned against him, savoring the feeling of his strong body and refusing to think about the future. He caressed her arm, and his slightly rough hand reminded her that he was a hard-working man, one whose strength came from chores rather than the gym. She loved that about him.

When the music started, it was with a wildly fast tune. Knox leaned close to her ear so that she could hear over the beat. "We'll dance to a song that isn't so rowdy. I'll teach you the Texas two-step."

She nodded. "Sounds good. I'd make a mess of it keeping up to this kind of song."

He laughed and kissed her temple.

She closed her eyes, reveling in the sensation of being in his embrace, of his gentle kiss. How had she lived without this for so long? How would she live without it when she left? Pain stabbed her heart, and she bit her lip. No, she wouldn't think of that tonight.

The right song soon began, and Knox rose to his feet. "Come on, cowgirl."

She smiled up at him. "I'm game." Rising to her feet, she put her arm around his waist. She'd go wherever this cowboy took her.

He had a strong lead, and in no time he had them sliding easily across the dance floor. She let herself go, enjoying the music and the magical experience of being in his arms.

They danced often, and she enjoyed getting to know Blake and Allison better. Except for when she was with Jessica, she couldn't remember when she'd ever had an evening like this, surrounded by genuine, kind people and enjoying conversation without looking for hidden barbs.

At one o'clock, Knox spoke near her ear, "Ready to hit the road?"

She nodded.

They said their goodbyes to Blake and Allison, who were staying on, and made their way to the truck.

On the way home, Knox held her hand in a tight grip, as if he didn't want to let her go. She had the same feeling. She didn't want the night to end. The bond she felt with him was so strong, so intimate, that it filled a need that had been raw for most of her life.

He kept glancing at her as he drove. She couldn't keep her gaze from him either.

When they got back to the house, he wrapped his arm around her and pulled her close as they walked to the front door. They entered quietly and walked silently toward their bedrooms.

She stopped at her door and turned to him. "Knox—"

He pulled her into his arms and kissed her fiercely. She wrapped her arms around his neck, wanting him, needing him. When he drew back, she said, "Give me ten minutes, then come to me."

He kissed her quickly again and nodded, his eyes slightly wild, his hands still holding her firmly against him.

It didn't take her long to freshen up and climb into bed. Knox slipped into the darkened room a couple of minutes later and strode toward her. She raised her arms, and he slid in beside her.

Cupping her face in his hand, he brushed a soft kiss across her lips. "Hey, beautiful. Is this a dream? Because it sure feels like it. The most amazing dream of my life."

She pulled him down, savoring the feeling of his body atop hers. "If it's a dream, I don't ever want to wake up."

He kissed her again, slowly, caressing her lips with his, slipping his tongue inside, exploring her. She sighed, sliding her hands along the muscles of his back, cherishing his strength.

He looked into her eyes. "I want to stay like this forever."

She smiled. "Please do."

He kissed her neck and slid tiny kisses to her ear. "I will if you will."

"Deal," she whispered.

He found that sensitive spot behind her ear and kissed it softly. She shivered. God, how she loved making love to this man.

He cupped her breast, his thumb caressing her swollen nipple. She sucked in a breath as tingles of desire swept through her. The man knew how to make her body sing. He took her nipple in his mouth and she almost cried out at the sensation. His fingers slid lightly down her belly, finding the cleft between her folds. He stroked her, and her thigh jerked at the intense pleasure he gave her.

She drew him to her and kissed him hard. "It's your turn tonight." She took him in her hand, admiring his full hardness. She pumped her fist up and down, and he gasped. She kept at it as she slid down in the bed.

She took him in her mouth, and he groaned. "Oh, God, Sadie!" She couldn't take all of him—he was too big. He clasped her face as she stroked him with her lips, loving the soft moans he made as she pleasured him. All at once, he grabbed her wrist. "Wait. Stop!"

She rose up, grabbed the condom she'd set out, and slipped it on him. He lay still, watching her with pleasure-glazed, half-closed eyes. She straddled him and he moaned, "Yes!" as she guided him inside her.

The feel of him filling her was amazing. He clasped her hips, urging her forward and then back, desire filling his eyes. She leaned toward him and grinned. "Who's your cowgirl now?"

"You are!"

Feeling wild and incredibly happy, she rode him hard, his strong hands at her hips connecting her to him in a powerful way. Suddenly he arched his head back and gasped, his body still and hard underneath her. He cried, "Sadie, oh God, Sadie!"

She gazed at him, her heart full, tenderness sweeping through her at the vulnerability on his face—at the beauty of him in the throes of his pleasure. She lay down on his chest. She'd never experienced anything like this—such joy, such peace, so much happiness—with another person.

Darkness waited at the back of her mind. The fact of her leaving. But that was for another night. This night was for sleeping in the arms of this very special man.

Opening the door quietly, she tiptoed out to the bathroom, then slid back in beside him. "Good night, Knox. I had a wonderful time tonight."

He turned over and stroked her cheek. "You're ready to go to sleep?"

She nodded.

"Come here, then. Let me hold you." She turned over, and he drew her against his chest. She closed her eyes and sighed. This was heaven. The black cloud that was her future? It couldn't rain on her tonight. She was warm and dry and safe in Knox's embrace.

SUNDAY MORNING, KNOX took a break from feeding the heifers in the barn pens and put in a call to Blake.

His friend answered after a few rings. "What's up? You missing me already?"

Knox laughed. "Not hardly. What's going on with you?"

"Nothing much, just driving in one of the pastures right now. Something wrong?"

Blake knew that Knox wasn't one for phone calls. "Nah." He wanted to talk about Sadie, but sharing his feelings didn't come naturally to him. "Jessica comes home on Friday."

"Really?"

"Yeah, that means Sadie won't be working with me anymore."

"Huh. I guess you'll kind of miss that."

"Yeah, I will. I mean, it's been nice having her along." Damn, he'd better just get it out. "I really like her." He heaved a sigh. "It's more than that, bro. I'm pretty sure I love her."

"Wow... That's something. I'm happy for you, Knox." He paused. "Wait. I'm assuming she loves you too? Has she decided that she's staying here?"

"That's the problem. I don't know if she loves me. I think she cares. She sure acts like it. But I'm sure she's still planning on going back to New York. Her whole life is there. Her amazing career, everything."

"Damn, Knox. That sucks."

He sighed. "Tell me about it. I don't know what to do. I've known from the beginning that she was going to leave, but I guess I just didn't want to think about it. Now that her leaving is almost here, I don't think I can handle it."

"Have you asked her to stay?"

Knox took his hat off and ran his fingers through his hair. "How the hell can I do that? How can I ask her to give up her multi-million-dollar job? Her whole life?"

"Holy shit! I didn't realize that she made that much."

Knox sighed. "She does. She's one of the best models in the world. Right at the top of her game."

Blake blew out a loud breath. "I get where you're coming from, man. What're you going to do?"

"I don't know. But the day she gets on that plane, it'll break my heart."

SADIE GLANCED AT MADDIE as they drove into Haskell. Knox's mom had insisted that Sadie come along to her ladies' quilting session this morning. She'd said that she wanted Sadie to meet her good friends.

Sadie had dressed in a casual outfit—an oversize, leopard-print silk shirt with matching pants that belled at the bottom. The group met at one of the quilters' homes, and most of the ladies were already there when Maddie and Sadie arrived. Maddie opened the SUV's back door and handed Sadie a large bag filled with her quilting supplies, then pulled out a covered baking pan.

When they got inside, the ladies stared at Sadie as if she were an exotic bird as Maddie introduced her. "This is Sadie. She's Jessica's friend from New York City—and I can tell you, my boy Knox thinks the world of her." Maddie beamed at Sadie, who smiled and nodded as the ladies gave her a warm welcome.

Maddie hooked her arm through Sadie's and headed into a hallway. She could feel every eye following them.

After setting the blueberry muffins she'd baked on the kitchen counter, Maddie said, "I've brought you something to quilt in my bag. Don't worry, I'll show you how."

Sadie glanced down at her hands. She'd never done anything remotely like sewing. She'd probably be terrible at it.

When they returned to the room, the ladies had rearranged
themselves, leaving two side-by-side chairs available for them.

Maddie handed Sadie a hoop with a pieced and pinned
quilt block in it. "Let me show you how to make your stitches,
honey. It's easy. You just have to take your time and pay attention."

Sadie watched as Maddie's fingers began making minute,
precise stitches around the pattern. When it was her turn, she
felt completely inadequate.

Maddie must have noticed her reluctance when she handed
her the needle, because she put her arm around her and gave a
gentle squeeze. "Look here, honey. Don't you worry a bit. You'll
do just fine. Try your best, and it'll be good enough."

Flushed with warmth from the other woman's gentle caring, Sadie made her first stitch. It wasn't so bad, and soon she
became comfortable holding the hoop and placing her stitches
to her satisfaction.

The low conversations going on around her soothed her
mind. She understood now why Maddie enjoyed coming here
so much. She couldn't help contrasting this experience with the
time she spent in her flat when she wasn't working, and her life
came up terribly wanting.

She sighed and pushed her needle through the fabric again.

"Something wrong, honey?" Maddie asked.

"No. This is such a lovely morning."

Maddie smiled. "It is, isn't it?"

Sadie smiled, but before she could say more, one of the
ladies asked, "What's it like to be a model?"

She tried to answer truthfully without being too much of a downer. More questions followed about where she lived and about her travels. She could tell that the ladies were enthralled at how exotic her life sounded.

They broke for refreshments, and Sadie asked questions of her own, learning about their lives and some of the projects the other women were working on. One young woman was repairing an amazing heirloom quilt made by her great-grandmother in the 1800s. Another was making a tiny baby quilt for her newest granddaughter, who was due in a few months. Many of the women were ranch wives, though some lived in the small town.

As she ate one of Maddie's delicious blueberry muffins and listened, Sadie's mind created a fantasy where she was a ranch wife, cooking for her hard-working husband and helping him on the ranch. Of course, that husband was Knox.

When it was time to go, everyone hugged her and she felt their welcome, the sense of belonging to this group of friends. It was precious.

On the way home, she looked out her window, silent and feeling a new sense of dread. How could she bear to leave this place? How could she return to the cold, unfeeling world of international modeling after being immersed in this sweet, loving life? Her eyes filled with tears.

Time was running out, and she had no choice. She had to leave. Soon.

Chapter Thirteen

Sadie took one last look in the bathroom mirror Friday night and tucked a stray lock of hair behind her ear. It was so wonderful to have Jessica home again. She and Maddie had worked together to prepare a welcome feast in her honor, and it had been a festive occasion. The only thing that had marred it for her was the knowledge that her days working with Knox had come to a close. She'd be spending the majority of her time now with Jessica.

He'd seemed to be thinking of that too, as his eyes had been more solemn than the festive occasion had called for. Maddie had certainly been happy to have her daughter back home, though. Once again, Sadie had imagined what her life would have been like if she'd had a caring mother like Maddie.

Jessica had brought home a nice bottle of Pinot Grigio, and when Sadie entered her bedroom, her friend had already poured a glass for each of them.

"Sit here, bestie." Jessica patted the bed beside her. "I'm so glad to be home. I want to hear all of the juicy details that I missed out on the past three weeks."

Sadie laughed. Though the two of them had spoken on the phone most nights, their conversations hadn't been in-depth. Jessica had been busy in the evenings with the new friends she'd made at the training course and the events organized for them.

Sadie settled back against the headboard. "You first. What all did you learn?"

Jessica launched into an excited and detailed description of the program she'd be leading once school started back up.

Sadie listened intently, amazed, as always, at her friend's intelligence and enthusiasm for teaching. When Jessica finally paused, Sadie said, "That sounds wonderful, and I know you'll be a fantastic leader of this program."

"Do you really think so?" Jessica's brow furrowed. "My principal has put such trust in me. I don't know what I'd do if I let him down. This whole thing is such a huge responsibility."

Sadie reached for her hand. "Are you kidding? Did you just listen to yourself? There's no way that's going to happen. You've got this, Jessica."

Her friend smiled. "Okay, maybe you're right. I worked really hard while I was gone. And there are a couple of people I can call on if I need help." She took a sip of wine. "Okay, now it's your turn. What's really up with you and my big brother?"

Sadie started by telling Jessica about going on the roundups and spending almost every day with Knox. "And when we went dancing, Jessica, it was so wonderful."

Her friend studied her for a few seconds, then grinned. "There's something you're not telling me."

Sadie looked down at her lap, feeling heat rise to her face—though why, she didn't know, since Jessica was her best friend. "You're right." She forced herself to meet Jessica's gaze. "We're sleeping together."

Jessica chuckled. "I knew it! Good for you. And good for Knox. My brother needed to get a life."

Sadie clenched her fist. "It's so damn complicated, though. The more I'm with him, the more I care for him. Jessica..." Eyes pleading, she looked at her best friend. "I don't know what to do. I'll have to go back any day now. How can I do that?" She swallowed and bowed her head. After a moment, she whispered, "But then, how can I not? My whole career is there."

Jessica slipped her arm around her shoulders. "Aww, I'm sorry I laughed. This is terrible. And I can tell Knox is feeling horrible, too. What can I do?"

Sadie shrugged. "I've been racking my brain, and I can't come up with anything. My agency will call me back any day. I don't know why it hasn't happened already." Tears slipped from the corners of her eyes.

Jessica pulled her closer. "Are you going to be okay?"

"I was so sure that I would be," she said quietly. After a moment, she wiped her face and raised her head. "Honestly, I'll have to be, won't I?" She met Jessica's gaze. "But I can't imagine going back to my old life and spending my awful, stressful days at work when I've experienced how wonderful a day with Knox can be."

Jessica frowned, her face full of pain for what her best friend faced. "Oh, honey."

THE NEXT MORNING, SADIE hung up the phone, shock reverberating through her system. Though she'd known the call would be coming, she hadn't been prepared. She had to go back. They'd been insistent on her returning right away. Only after extensive haggling had she won an agreement to be back the following Monday morning. Her hands trembled as she finished getting dressed.

A moment later, she knocked on Jessica's bedroom door.

"Come in," Jessica called in a sleepy voice.

Sadie slipped inside and sat on the edge of the bed. "I got the call."

Jessica jerked to a sitting position. "What did they say?"

"I fought them. I have until next Monday to show up at the agency." Her face crumpled, and she reached for her friend. "How can I go back to my life after being here? Everything's so wonderful. And, Knox... How can I leave him?" A sob escaped before she bit down on her bottom lip.

Jessica held her tight. "I know, honey. I know." After a long moment, she said, "This calls for a girls' day." She reached for her phone, and within minutes she had manicures, pedicures, and massages booked for them both. "Now, put next Monday out of your mind. We have the better part of a week to enjoy ourselves, and we're going to make the most of it." Then she gave her another hug. "And, when you tell my brother, you tell him that as well. You two make every minute you have together count, you hear me?"

Sadie wiped her eyes and smiled. "I will."

DURING HER NAIL APPOINTMENT, she had them done in her usual fashion, the way she wore them for work, and it nearly broke her heart. It was like her first goodbye to the ranch.

After their relaxing massages, Jessica drove them to dinner, where the first thing they did was order margaritas. Jessica clinked her glass with Sadie's. "To best friends and making every moment count."

Sadie smiled. "I love you." After taking a sip, she sighed. "This has been a wonderful day. I was almost able to forget about leaving."

"Good. It's working, then." After taking another swallow of her frozen drink, Jessica said, "I still can't believe that I had to be gone for most of your trip. That totally sucks. I'm going to miss you something awful when you go back."

Sadie smiled. "It did stink. But I'll send you a ticket and you can come see me. Maybe over Christmas break? Central Park is gorgeous then, remember? We can go ice-skating."

Jessica grinned. "That sounds amazing." Then she raised an eyebrow. "Or you could come back."

Knox's face flashed before her, and pain stabbed her heart. Would he even care about her by Christmastime? "We'll see."

"One thing's for sure; we need to do a better job of keeping in touch when you go back. Agreed?" She held out her hand.

Sadie grinned and shook with her. "Agreed, bestie."

On the way home, she leaned her head back and sighed. Now she faced the hard part. She had to break the news to Knox.

SATURDAY NIGHT, KNOX sat next to Sadie at dinner, rather than across from her, holding her hand under the linen tablecloth. He desperately needed to be close to her. It was their last night together, and he'd booked a hotel room. He was taking her to the airport early the next morning. Sunday traffic would be light, so they wouldn't have to rush.

They'd made love every night since the phone call from Sadie's agency. He'd gone to her room after the house was dark and quiet, and their loving had been fierce and desperate.

Earlier in the evening, Sadie had said her tearful goodbyes to his sister and parents, and she was still solemn as she sat next to him.

He squeezed her hand. "Hungry?"

Her lip trembled. "Not really."

He scooted back his chair and crouched next to her, putting his arm around her shoulders. "Honey, I just hate this."

She nodded, but didn't say anything. Maybe she couldn't.

The waitress came and brought their drinks, then took their orders.

He sat down again, but kept hold of her hand. He didn't try any more conversation. She seemed to need the silence.

They said little during dinner. Conversation seemed so unimportant in contrast to the magnitude of her leaving.

It was a quiet ride to the hotel room.

He undressed her with gentle hands, and she smiled at him as tears leaked from her eyes. He kissed them from her cheeks and, when she was naked, he carried her to bed.

A moment later, he slid in beside her and took her into his arms.

She wrapped her arm around his waist and nestled her head on his chest. "This is how I want to remember you," she whispered.

"I'll remember every moment of this night, honey." He leaned his cheek against her and sighed.

She wrapped her leg around his. It felt perfect and natural, and he wanted to freeze the moment in time so that he'd always have it to come back to. Her skin was so soft. He slid his fingers up her arm and caressed her shoulder. "Sadie, I know I've told you this before, but you're beautiful. You're exquisite in every way. And not just on the outside where everyone can see. You have a beautiful soul."

She sighed so deeply that he was surprised her lungs could hold so much air. "Knox, I've never felt this way about anyone. You're the most amazing person I've ever met. You're kind and caring and so smart. You're gentle—and yet you're incredibly strong." She ran her hand over his chest. "You have a beautiful body. I noticed that right off, even though I could tell that you didn't like me at all."

He laughed. "You got under my skin pretty fast, though. It didn't take me long to figure out that there was more to you than I first thought." He caressed her cheek. "I'll never be able to sleep alone again. There's going to be a big ol' empty spot beside me from now on."

"Oh, Knox!" She buried her face in his chest, and he cradled her head in his palm. When he heard her suck in a breath, he tilted her face to him and kissed her gently. "Now, no tears. This is our last night together."

She nodded. "You're right. Make love to me." She kissed him softly. "And I'll make love to you. We'll remember it always, okay?"

He rolled her on her back. "Always." He kissed her, long and slow. Tonight, he'd make her body sing. She'd feel so freaking amazing that she'd forget all about catching that plane in the morning. He nibbled her neck, and she laughed. He whispered in her ear, "Get ready for some good lovin', honey."

"Ready, handsome!"

And, damn, did he keep his promise.

THE STRICKEN LOOK ON Sadie's face when the alarm went off said it all. Knox pulled her into his arms and hugged her tight. She sobbed quietly. He whispered in her ear, wishing he could do something to ease her pain, but knowing that nothing would help. In a short time, they'd be parted—and it might as well be for forever. His life was here in Texas, and hers was in New York and in a million other places all over the world.

He kissed her temple and continued to murmur to her. After a while, he kissed her cheek. "We have to get up, sweetheart. You need to dress. We can't miss your flight."

She nodded, but didn't take her arm from around him.

He sighed and kissed her again before sitting up.

She sniffed and sat up too. "You're right. It won't take me long. I don't give a crap what I look like."

He chuckled. "What about your fans?"

She made a face. "They can suck it."

He burst out laughing. "Wow. Okay."

She laughed quietly. "I don't really mean that. But seriously, I'm not going to do much. I just can't face it."

True to her word, fifteen minutes later, she zipped up her suitcase. Her hanging bag was ready too.

He pulled her into a hug. "We'll have time for a quick breakfast."

She shook her head. "I couldn't."

"Okay, we won't, then."

A quiet sob escaped her lips, and his arms tightened around her. When she eventually drew back, he tilted her face so he could meet her gaze. "We'll text every morning and call each other every night."

She nodded and wiped her face. "Right."

She gripped his hand fiercely on the way to the airport. They found a parking spot, and he carried her bags to the check-in counter. They had plenty of time before her boarding call.

It didn't take them long to check her luggage, and then there was nothing else to do. He led her to security, her grip on his hand like a vise. When he could go no farther, he stopped.

Her eyes were dark with pain. He pulled her into his arms. She clung to him with surprising strength. "Call me when you get home. Promise?" he said quietly.

He felt her nod. When she pulled back, he kissed her, putting his whole heart into it. "Sadie, I'll miss you more than I have words for."

She covered her mouth as tears sprang to her eyes.

He turned and strode away, knowing that staying any longer would just make it worse for her. He shut his ears, afraid he'd hear her sob. With no real future for their relationship, he had no idea when, or if ever, he'd see Sadie again.

Chapter Fourteen

S adie stood still, her gaze wandering over the pale furniture, the glass walls, and all of the other beautiful things in her flat that used to give her such comfort. This homecoming was far different from the ones that she'd so looked forward to in her past. Her home had always given her an immediate sense of contentment, of peace, and she'd always begun to relax the moment she'd set foot through her door.

This evening, her place felt cold, sterile, and so very lonely. After the warm colors and comfortable country décor of the McKinnis ranch house, she could finally see her home for what it was...a status symbol. Her interior designer had put together a place that befitted her lifestyle—chic, worldly, cutting-edge. She realized now that this wasn't who she was. Knox had helped her discover the real woman inside the internationally famous supermodel persona that she presented to the world.

She tossed her hanging bag over what passed for a sofa and rolled her case into the bedroom. Quickly shedding her clothes, she headed in to shower. Memories of Knox filled her thoughts as she washed away the grimy feeling she always had after traveling. Instead of comforting her, though, the memories were like sharp arrows of pain in her chest. Knowing that their lives were now separated by nearly two thousand miles, the emptiness in her chest was nearly unbearable.

After her shower, she realized that she'd forgotten to text Knox that she'd arrived safely. She went to the kitchen and poured herself a glass of slightly sweet rosé before heading to the chair that faced the bank of windows overlooking the park. The lights had all come on outside while she was in the shower. She used to love this view, but now, comparing it to the beauty of the Texas ranch, it seemed sad in comparison. *Is everything about my life ruined now?* She sighed, her chest heavy with grief, and took a sip from her glass.

After a moment, she picked up her phone, but instead of texting Knox, she pressed call.

He answered on the first ring. "Sadie? Are you home safe?"

She cradled the phone close to her ear, as if pressing her cheek to Knox's chest. "I'm just fine. How are you?"

He was silent for a moment. "I miss you. I hate it that you're not here."

Her heart panged, and she swallowed past the lump in her throat. "I miss you too. I feel like I'm in a stranger's house. How could I ever have thought that my place was beautiful?"

Knox chuckled, though it sounded sad. "Texas will do that to a person."

She smiled. Spoken like a true Texan.

"Have you eaten yet?" Knox asked, his voice heavy with concern. She'd been unable to eat much the past couple of days.

"No, I just got out of the shower."

"Promise me that you'll order something. You've got to be strong for your first day back at work tomorrow."

Hearing those words sent a wave of anxiety rushing through her. She'd dreaded the thought of returning to work since she'd received the call from her agency. "I will. I promise."

Lord, nothing sounded even remotely palatable. But she'd keep her word.

"So, how was your flight?"

"A little bumpy after we left Dallas, then the plane gained altitude and it calmed down. It was long and boring. I don't know what I'd do if I couldn't fly first class. The seats are packed so tightly together in coach that my legs have nowhere to go." She hoped that he wouldn't think she was a snob. It was about comfort.

He laughed. "With those gorgeous long legs, I'm sure that's a problem."

She smiled at his description. "It is. I fly a lot, and sitting cramped would really become a problem. My legs and feet take enough of a beating in my profession already."

He sighed. "I wish I could see you work sometime."

She laughed quietly. "You'd get bored. Seriously, it's just a bunch of mostly women prancing around in different clothes for hours on end." Even though their lives as a couple would never work, would it be so wrong if he came to see her? They'd decided that being friends was the only long-term option they had. Friends could visit each other, right? But wouldn't that just bring them both more pain when they had to say goodbye again?

He barked a laugh. "That's a terrible description of what you do, and you know it." After a pause, he said, "You're one of the best, and I'd love to watch you in action, Sadie. I really would."

She imagined having him in the audience as she walked the runway and realized that she'd like it too. "Thanks for being interested in my work. It's sweet. Maybe you can do that some-day."

"Of course I'm interested. It's part of who you are. I'd love to come watch you."

The hope in his voice was obvious. Pain stabbed her chest. Why did their lives have to be so different? Knox was born to be a cowboy, and he loved his beautiful Texas ranch. He had no place in her world. She'd worked her whole life to reach the top tier of her career; a career that supported her in a way that most people only dreamed of. Her place was here, in this world, do-ing that job. She and Knox would always be apart.

Devastation hit her like a brick wall. She could no longer hold it at bay. Tears leaked from her eyes, and she slumped down in her seat, suddenly lacking the strength to hold her head up.

She whispered, "I need to make this an early night. Good night, Knox."

"Rest well, honey. Good night."

That "honey" was her undoing. Painful sobs racked her chest.

When she found herself calm again, she felt limp, unable to move as hopelessness overwhelmed her. Turning her head, she gazed outside. A black pit opened inside her as she imagined her days ahead. Lonely days, hectic days. Days without Knox in them.

The dark room allowed her mind to roam back to the won-derful weeks that she'd spent with the kind, gentle cowboy. She wrapped her arms around herself. She wouldn't think about the future. She wouldn't think about tomorrow. Knox would fill her dreams tonight. That would have to be enough.

BLAKE ENDED THE JOKE at Ryder's expense with a hearty slap on his back. Knox glanced over at them and smiled. His gaze wandered around the tiny bar, which was situated a couple of miles outside of Haskell. The place held only three small tables and had five seats at the old plywood bar. It had been their favorite hangout when he and his friends had first achieved drinking age. Ranchers were the main patrons, coming in after a long day on a tractor or working cattle.

He met the gaze of the old man at the end of the bar and nodded. He was a fellow rancher who'd weathered multiple droughts and economic downturns and was still raising cattle to this day. *Will I still be ranching when I'm his age?* Then he thought of living all that time without Sadie, and his heart fell.

"You ready for another beer?" Josh called out.

Knox downed the last of the one in front of him. "Yep." He wanted to drown the pain in his chest that never let up; to quiet the relentless thoughts in his head. His three friends had set up this evening hoping to cheer him up, and Blake had picked him up in his truck so that Knox wouldn't be responsible for driving. He could let go and unleash the agony of his desperate need for Sadie, surrounded by the safe companionship of his friends.

Blake leaned close and asked quietly, "How're you doing?"

Without hesitation, he answered, "I'm gut-shot."

His other friends heard him and grew quiet. The worried looks on their faces made him feel guilty for ruining their fun.

Blake put his arm across Knox's shoulders. "I'm so sorry. I wish I could help."

Knox took a long swallow of beer as Blake released him. "I know her career is in New York and that she travels all over the world for her job. There's no place for me in her life." He sighed and ran his palm across his forehead. "I just don't know how to live without her. My heart... It's ruined for any other woman."

"Drink up," Ryder said. "We're here for you, bro."

"Damn straight." Josh raised his beer to Knox.

Knox nodded. "Thanks. It means a lot."

As his friends started up a conversation, his heart felt so heavy he wondered how it stayed in place.

Later, when he was more than a little the worse for wear from the beers his friends had kept buying him, Blake drove him home. His friend squeezed his shoulder when they pulled up at the ranch. "I'm here for you, anytime, day or night. Hang in there, Knox."

Knox nodded—but the thing was, he didn't know how to do that.

SADIE TURNED TOWARD the camera and smiled seductively, trying to make the sexy emotion reach her eyes. Belize was hot and muggy, and she'd been posing in this tiny swimsuit in the shallow waves for hours. Sand seemed to have invaded every crevice of her body. This shoot was for the Sports Illustrated Swimsuit Edition, and she had a good shot at making the cover.

The sun beat down on her as she struck another pose, the warm water in the small bay doing nothing to cool her off. It was a beautiful setting with palm trees and flowering bushes farther from the water, but it all meant nothing to her. All she could think of was Knox and how much she missed him.

"Sadie?" The photographer lowered his camera. "I said stand up."

"Oh, sorry." Dammit, she needed to pay attention. She couldn't afford to have her mind constantly flipping back to Texas. But, night and day, Knox was never far from her thoughts.

"Now, show me that sexy smile of yours, baby."

She looked over her shoulder, giving a sensuous smile for the camera. She could do this stuff in her sleep. The trick was making her smile reach her eyes, inviting the viewer close. This was what had brought her prosperity and fame. She cranked up the come-hither to the next level and changed her pose. *Only now my heart isn't in it.*

Everything about her career rubbed her raw. The travel, the hectic rushing around, the posing for hours on end. It all seemed so pointless, somehow. Only Knox held any meaning for her. She shook her long hair back from her shoulders. *Come on, Sadie. Pay attention, dammit.*

She dug deep and focused on the camera lens, making love to it, allowing nothing else to exist.

"That's it, baby. You're amazing. You're gorgeous. Just like that. Show me some more." The camera clicked and clicked again.

At last, the photographer called, "That's it, Sadie. You were great. Always a pleasure working with you."

A crew member handed her a towel as she strode from the water. Sand abraded her skin as she dried off. Exhausted, she found her driver and headed back to the hotel. After a long shower where it seemed to take forever to rid herself of the rough sand, she threw on a robe and called room service for a bottle of Pinot Noir.

Her room had a stunning ocean view, but she didn't have the heart to enjoy it. She glanced at the time. Belize was an hour earlier than Texas. Knox was probably still working.

The wine arrived, and she poured herself a glass. In a comfortable, overstuffed chair covered in bright tropical material, she tucked her feet under her and called him.

"Sadie? I thought you were working today."

She couldn't help but smile. The sound of his deep, masculine voice gave her such joy that she laid her hand over her heart. "I worked all day today, but I'm done now. What are you doing?"

"I just got back from running some errands in Haskell. The usual stuff." She could hear the smile in his voice when he said, "I never buy Sports Illustrated, but now I can't wait for the Swimsuit Edition to come out. My sweetheart's going to be on the cover."

She laughed. *"Maybe* I'll be on the cover. There's stiff competition for that honor." She could hardly believe how happy she was after feeling so depressed all day.

"There's no contest. You'll get it. You're the most gorgeous woman in the world."

Her heart sang with joy. Knox did that to her so easily. "Thanks for believing in me."

"So, where did they shoot the pictures of you?"

"It was miserable. I was in water about a foot deep with waves washing over me for hours and hours. Sand got all over me—and when I say all over me, use your imagination."

He cracked up. "I'm using it, and that sounds very uncomfortable."

"It was. Try looking sexy with that mess going on."

"Modeling isn't an easy job, is it?"

She sighed. Talking to Knox was amazing. It was like coming home, something she never felt in her flat anymore.

When she said goodbye at last, it nearly broke her heart, as it did every time she hung up with him. It was like leaving Texas all over again. The same heartache, the same sure knowledge that she'd never be with him again.

True, they could fly in to see each other, but what would be the point? It would make them both incredibly miserable to say goodbye again. Knox couldn't live in New York, and she couldn't make her living in Texas. So many of her shoots happened in the city. New York was one of the world's major fashion centers. Their life together just wouldn't work.

She needed to quit focusing on what she couldn't have. That was the smart thing to do. But her heart was having no such thing.

She sat before the windows and watched the sunset fade to night, miserable and lonely and, more than anything, out of hope.

She went to bed without dinner and lay there, her mind numb and her heart aching. Her text tone sounded and she reached for her phone. Heart speeding with joy, she saw it was Knox. He wrote:

My heart aches for you. There's a hole in my chest that nothing can fill. You're the first thing I think of when I wake up, and you'll be the last thing I think of before I fall asleep. Sadie, you're everything to me. Sweet dreams.

She drew the phone to her chest and held it against her heart as slow tears seeped from her eyes. She had a cavern inside her, too, and its name was Knox.

KNOX, EYES FIXED ON the calf, backed his big gelding into the roping box. With a quick nod to Jason at the head gate, he waited for the calf to explode from the chute before his horse bolted out of the box.

He missed his catch and groaned out loud. His mind just wasn't focused on business tonight. Ryder, Josh and Blake catcalled good-naturedly at his miss as he rode back to join them.

"Take your head out, bro. That calf wasn't even fast," Blake said with a grin.

Knox rolled his eyes. "I should kick my own ass."

Blake laughed and entered the box. A moment later, he burst out in pursuit of his calf and had him roped and tied in seconds.

When he threw his hands in the air to signal time, he called, "Now that's how you do it, bro!"

"Asshole," Knox called and grinned. But his luck only got worse. He missed more than he caught that round, and he knew it was because his mind was on something—someone—else.

When they stopped to let the horses blow, Knox strode to the end of the arena and put in a call to Sadie. He breathed a sigh of relief when she answered.

"Knox, I'm so glad you called."

"We're taking a break between pens, and I wanted to talk to you." He loved the low, sexy, tone of her voice and how it made his heart speed up.

"I wish I were there. I can just imagine it—the arena dust floating in the air after a run, the bawling of the calves in the pen, and how you guys joke with each other." She paused. "God, Knox, I'm so homesick for you. I know that's weird since the ranch isn't my home, but I've never felt more at home anywhere in the world."

"Oh, Sadie. Honey, this here's my home, but something's missing now. And that something is you. I used to feel whole here, like this was the only place I'd ever want to be. But that's not true anymore. There's someplace I want to be at even more—and that's with you." Just saying the words sent a stabbing pain to his heart. He knew that being with her wouldn't happen.

Her voice low and filled with sadness, she said, "I know what you mean. I used to love having a day off between shoots. But today was miserable. With nothing to keep me busy at my place, I spent my whole day missing you."

"God, honey, we're a mess." He turned and looked back at the roping box. The guys were all drinking beers and talking. He had a little more time. "So, do you work tomorrow?"

He listened quietly, absorbing the sweetness of her voice as she talked about her next job. He could stand here all night and listen to her talk, because that would mean that he never had to say goodbye. Letting her go was a new heartbreak every night, and he dreaded it.

When he glanced back again, the guys were mounting up. "I've got to get back to my horse, sweetheart. I'll think of you tonight. I always do."

"Oh, Knox. I hate saying goodbye."

"So do I, honey. So do I."

When he got back to his horse, Blake asked, "Was that Sadie?"

Knox nodded. "She said to tell you boys hi."

Josh called out, "Hell, yeah. Too bad you saw her first, buddy."

Ryder laughed. "In your dreams, man. Knox is way better-looking than you."

Josh cracked up. "Not what the ladies say."

Knox grinned. He didn't know what he'd do without his friends and their support.

Late that night, as he lay in bed, he texted Sadie.

I dreamed of you last night. We were married, and I'd built my home here on the ranch. We were sitting on the front porch watching the sunset. It seemed so real, honey. This awful hole in my gut was gone, and I was so happy. You're my dream girl, Sadie. My heart will never let you go.

He set the phone on the nightstand and stared into the dark. They couldn't be together, but he would never be happy apart.

Chapter Fifteen

Sadie stared out the cab window at the dreary, rain-drenched streets of Tribeca, still snarled with the aftermath of rush-hour traffic. Her day had been long and exhausting and, as with every other shoot since her return to New York, her heart hadn't been in it. The streetlights would come on soon. Maybe they would usher out her dismal attitude along with the decidedly grim essence of the late afternoon.

Her phone rang, and seeing Jessica's name on her screen lightened Sadie's mood immediately. "Hi, it's good to hear your voice. It's been a hell of a day."

"I'm glad I caught you!" Jessica said, with her usual enthusiasm. "So tell me why it was an awful day, honey."

Sadie sighed and leaned back against the cab's cracked vinyl seat. "I got up before dawn this morning to get ready for my shoot. It was planned for outdoors, and the weather called for rain in the afternoon. Though this morning had plenty of sun, the photographer was stressed and wanted to rush things while the weather held. Then the wind picked up and made things difficult, but we worked through it. After the clouds moved in, the crew had to set up more lights, and that took time. I thought the photographer would to have a heart attack."

She paused as memories flooded her mind. "Jessica, all I think about is Knox. Keeping my mind on my work is so hard."

"Oh, honey. I wish there was something I could do."

Sadie sighed again. "I know, and I appreciate it. There just isn't." She took a deep breath, determined to be more upbeat. "Anyway, we finished the shoot just as the rain started, so it all worked out. I got drenched waiting on a cab, though. My people didn't order a car for this afternoon—an oversight that I'm going to address. But enough about me. Tell me all about your day."

In an excited voice, Jessica told Sadie how, now that school had started, the other teachers were throwing themselves into the new initiative with wholehearted enthusiasm.

Sadie listened intently, making appropriate comments and wanting to be happy for her friend. Deep down, though, nothing made her happy anymore. As Jessica wound down, Sadie said, "I'm so glad everything is going so well. You've worked hard to make this project a success. I know your principal must be happy with what you've accomplished so far."

"Oh, he is. He came into the teachers' lounge yesterday at lunch and bragged on me in front of everyone. It really made me feel good."

"That's fantastic—and well deserved. You're the best, Jessica. Don't you forget it." Jessica's job meant everything to her, and Sadie was truly glad that she was finally getting the recognition that she deserved.

"Okay, so enough small talk. Tell me how you're really doing, bestie. We haven't talked about this since you first came home. Did you ever make that appointment with your therapist?" Jessica asked.

"Yes, I did." She had gone, once, but she hadn't made the requested follow-up appointment. Talking about what she was going through had seemed so pointless.

"And?" Jessica wasn't going to let this go.

"I went, and we talked. Like I said, there's no answer to this." The cab slowed as it came to her building. She held the phone between her shoulder and ear and grabbed her wallet out of her purse.

"Well, what did he say about your depression? It's worse, isn't it?"

Sadie handed the fare across the seat back to the driver and opened her door. "He asked how my medication was working, and I mentioned how I was feeling. He told me that I could increase my dose by adding an extra half a pill a day, and then said to call if that didn't help."

"What? He didn't want you to schedule a follow-up?"

Dammit. Having a bossy friend could be a real pain. "Actually, he did, but I didn't make one." Rain pelted Sadie's head as she dashed for the front door of her building. The doorman opened it for her, and she rushed inside.

"Sadie Stewart, you're going to call first thing in the morning and set up that appointment. And, you're going to start taking that extra dose. Do you hear me?" Jessica was using that no-nonsense voice that Sadie knew so well.

Sadie groaned quietly. "Okay, bossy. I will." The air-conditioning in the lobby chilled her to the bone as she waited for the elevator to arrive.

"I'll be calling you for a progress report, so don't think that you can just sweep this under the rug, girl."

"Oh, I wouldn't think of it."

After a short pause, Jessica said quietly, "You're not the only one who's struggling. Knox is having a bad time of it. I've never seen him like this. Mom says that he's not coming in for lunch, and he won't let her pack him one. He says he's not hungry. He works late in the evenings and tells Mom to leave his dinner plate on the stove. We hardly see him anymore. It's like he's withdrawn inside himself to some dark place. I'm worried about him."

Each word Jessica spoke sent pain shooting to Sadie's heart. Why hadn't she considered the impact that her leaving would have on Knox? She'd only been thinking of *her* loss, *her* pain. She'd been oblivious to his suffering. How could she have been so selfish?

The sweet scent of the lilies on the lobby table under an ornate mirror sent nausea swirling in her stomach. Feeling sicker by the second, she teetered on her four-inch heels in the thick carpet and swallowed hard against her constricted throat.

"My God, Jessica. I had no idea. Why didn't you tell me?" She should never have gone to Texas. She should never have turned Knox's life upside down.

Her friend sighed. "Because I knew you were suffering too. Why would I want to make you feel worse? But since he's doing so badly right now, I figured that I should say something. I know how much you care about him."

"Thank you for telling me. Of course I wanted to know." It came to her then. She knew what she had to do. It was the only thing that she *could* do for him.

She didn't even remember telling Jessica goodbye, but as she entered the elevator, she realized that she had ended the call and was slipping her phone into her purse. Chilled and desolate beyond tears, she sank into a mental void.

A short time later, snuggled under her covers in a warm nightgown, she let go. Loss hit her like a ten-story building. Breath whooshed from her lungs. She didn't try to protect herself. Didn't push back against the weight pressing her into the mattress, stealing her strength, darkening her mind. This was how it would be from now on. But that was okay. She would be protecting Knox, and that was all that mattered.

She lay there, pummeled by the storm of her despair, buried under the weight of her loss, until she knew that Knox would have finished his late supper. She wouldn't call. Wouldn't let him argue with her. She feared the part of her that was weak; the part of her that might give in to his pleading when he heard what she had to say. Instead, she texted:

Knox, I've realized that what we're doing is hurting you terribly, and I can't do that anymore. We both know that our relationship has no future. You need to let me go. You need to move on with your life. All I want is for you to be happy. I wish I had never come to Texas! Talking on the phone and texting each other only prolongs something that is going nowhere and a relationship that is causing you pain. Knox, I will never hurt you again! You know that I care about you, and that's why I'm doing this. Please believe me when I say this is the hardest thing I've ever done. I won't contact you anymore, and I don't want you to contact me. I wish you a wonderful life. Sadie

Her phone rang. It was Knox. She ignored it. It took a while, then her voicemail tone sounded. It was obviously a long message.

A moment later he texted:

You absolutely can't do this, Sadie! Of course we need to stay in touch! How can you even suggest this? Don't you know how much you mean to me? I'm calling again. Answer your damn phone!

Her phone rang again. She let it ring.

He texted again:

Dammit Sadie! This is pissing me off! I won't cut off contact with you! Answer me, for God's sake!

Her phone rang again. She didn't answer.

She sent:

Knox, my mind is made up. Please know that I care for you more than I've cared for any man I've ever known. That's why I'm doing this. Don't call me and don't text me. I want you to heal from this hurt that we're both feeling. I want you to have a happy life.

She paused after she hit send, dreading typing the next words as a sob escaped her lips.

I want you to meet a woman from Texas. One who can share your beautiful world. Someone who can live on your ranch and give you beautiful children. That's my dream for you. Goodbye, sweet Knox. I'll never forget you.

He sent back:

My God, Sadie. Don't do this. Please, please, don't do this.

She turned her phone to silent and set it on the nightstand. Suddenly her pent-up emotions broke free. She cradled a pillow to her chest and cried loud, racking sobs, her chest aching harder with each one.

Her phone vibrated against the glass tabletop as Knox called again and again. She covered her ear with a pillow to block the sound, unable to bear the fact that she was causing him yet more pain on this dark night.

Though her own heart was breaking, she knew deep down that she was right. This was the only way that Knox could heal. Somehow, she'd find a way to live with it.

THE FOLLOWING MORNING, Knox sped down the bumpy pasture road, his thoughts scattered like the strong breeze that blew through the lacy mesquite trees. A storm was due later in the afternoon. He'd texted Sadie first thing this morning when she didn't answer his call. She'd responded right away, but not with anything he wanted to hear, reiterating only that they couldn't communicate anymore. *Dammit.* He refused to accept that it was over between them. He couldn't bear it.

When he pulled up to the gate to the next pasture, he texted Jessica, too upset to care that she was in class.

Sis, Sadie has cut off all communication between us. Says that she's hurting me by continuing our relationship. That's total bull-shit! Can you please get hold of her and talk some sense into her? I'm dying here.

It took a few minutes, then Jessica answered:

After school, I'll get in touch with her. But, hey, I need to do what's best for Sadie, okay?

His heart thumped hard against his chest wall. What was best for Sadie? Did his sister mean that his cutting off communication with Sadie might be best for her?

He leaned his forehead against the steering wheel as shock reverberated through his system. Was he being a selfish asshole? Was this decision the right thing for the woman he cared more for than anything else in the world?

He got out and opened the gate, stunned at the concept—and with an inkling that truth lay at the center of it.

He drove through, then got out and closed the gate, all while his mind circled around the notion of never talking to Sadie again.

As he searched the pasture for the cattle, he considered the fact that he'd only been thinking of himself, of his own pain, of his own loss. Sure, he'd worried about how Sadie was doing while they'd talked and texted, but he'd never considered the fact that keeping in touch with her could be what was making her miserable.

He eventually found the herd and, as he poured feed out for them, he continued to mull over what Sadie was going through. He recalled why she'd come to Texas in the first place and realized that she was right back in the thick of that unhappy career again. He considered how missing him might be making the stress of her career so much worse.

He moved on to the next pasture and his stomach, acidic for days, began to burn like fire. His mother had put her foot down that morning and insisted that he make it back to the house for lunch. He'd finally agreed after he'd seen the hurt in her face the third time he'd said no.

But when he came in for lunch, he found that she'd made chili and cornbread, and his stomach rebelled at the first bite of the spicy food. He hurriedly buttered a slice of cornbread and ate it to cushion the lining of his belly. Cold milk helped too. After a couple more slices of cornbread, he ate several more spoonfuls of chili—enough to make his mother happy. When she left the kitchen, he scraped the rest into the trashcan. His mind, meanwhile, had been working overtime. He was certain, now, that going along with Sadie's plan was the right thing to do—but for her, not for him. If he complied, his heart would never heal.

He went back out to his truck, but before he turned the key in the ignition, he texted Jessica:

Sis, don't talk to Sadie. I realize now that I've only been hurting her by keeping up our relationship. She's right. We need to stop this, now. I'll let her know that she's right. After that, I won't be calling her or texting her anymore.

Not long after, Jessica sent:

I'm sorry, brother, I know how much this hurts. I love you.

The truck roared to life as his heart began to die. A darkness like nothing he'd ever experienced descended on his soul.

IN THE WEEKS SINCE her decision to cut off all contact with Knox, Sadie had lived a nightmare of her own making. Sleeping very little at night and experiencing a complete loss of appetite meant that pounds that she could ill afford to lose had been stripped from her already slender frame. Her agent had given her a stern talking-to, so much so that she'd taken Sadie to lunch and had sat with her until Sadie had eaten the better portion of her meal.

Now Sadie held onto the polished rail of the megayacht and gazed out to the horizon. She was in St. Lucia for a fashion shoot, and her agent had insisted she attend this influential billionaire's on-board party. She was completely exhausted—certainly too tired to enjoy the caviar and expensive champagne that were just a few of the many items on offer this sunny afternoon at sea.

People dressed in skimpy outfits strolled along the deck, drinks in hand, or conversed in small groups as sexily dressed waitresses armed with trays of drinks or hors d'oeuvres flitted among them.

Her solitude abruptly ended when a distinguished man in his fifties walked up beside her. "You look lonely over here all by yourself."

Ugh. Why couldn't men leave her alone? "I'm not. I was actually enjoying the peace and quiet."

He extended a glass of champagne. "You look thirsty. The sun's a beast, isn't it?"

"No thanks. I'm not drinking today." She turned away, hoping he'd get the hint. Instead, he leaned on the railing beside her as though he planned on staying a while. She'd leave, except that this was the only quiet place she'd been able to find on the deck.

He took a drink from his glass. "So, do you know George?"

She glanced at him. "Our host?"

The corner of his mouth quirked up. "If you don't, it's okay. A lot of people are here just to party."

She shook her head. "I'm here on business, actually. My agent suggested that I come."

The man raised his brows. "Your agent?" He thrust out his hand. "Brent Cross, by the way."

She nodded without shaking his hand. "Sadie." No way was she telling him her full name, just in case he recognized it. This was becoming a pain in the ass. She thrust away from the rail. "Nice to meet you, Mr. Cross."

"Hey, don't run off."

She ignored him and strode toward the other end of the deck. A distant movement caught her attention. A boat was approaching. She looked around; the bosun had noticed it too. Sadie moved to the railing, her eyes never leaving the vessel. It was coming in fast, and something about it bothered her.

She glanced at the other guests. Nobody else appeared to have noticed. The bosun spoke into his radio, and a waitress near Sadie had stopped and was staring fixedly at the incoming boat. Then she took a hesitant step, her eyes wide. Alarmed at her reaction, Sadie headed toward the bosun, but before she reached him, he bounded up the nearby stairs to an upper deck.

The vessel was closer now, and Sadie could see a group of men clustered on the deck. Were they masked? She couldn't make out their faces. Were they locals? Maybe she was worried for nothing.

She searched the groups on deck until she found George whatever-his-name-was. She made her way toward him just as a bulked-up man in a crew uniform appeared at his side and took him by the arm.

Turning around, she caught sight of the bosun, now armed, as he began ushering guests toward the stairs. An announcement came over the air. "We have an unidentified vessel approaching. Please proceed to the upper deck immediately. Quickly now."

But when she looked back, George was heading belowdecks. *What the hell?*

As she rushed toward the stairs, the boat reached the stern, where the deck was lowest. It was the spot where swimmers entered the water on a megayacht like this. She cried out as shots boomed from that direction.

The bosun yelled, "Hurry!"

The billionaire was already out of sight below.

People screamed in fear, and Sadie took the remaining stairs two at a time.

Before she made it inside the upper deck, however, more shots rang out and a heavily accented male voice shouted, "Stop!"

She looked back. At least fifteen other passengers crowded behind her. A man from the other vessel, armed with some kind of rifle, stood near the stairs which led up from the stern. More men appeared as she watched. Her heart beat like a battering ram against her chest wall, and she couldn't catch her breath.

The man waved his rifle. "Come! Everybody!"

The bosun, outgunned by the armed men, walked quietly with them toward the man who had shouted.

One of the pirates—for it was now clear that that was what they were—came forward and grabbed the bosun's gun.

The man who appeared to be the leader said in his strongly accented voice, "Jewelry off. Watches. Everything."

Another man carrying a bag made his way through the crowd, stopping at each person. When he stood before her, his eyes were cold, unfeeling. She had no doubt that he'd kill her if she didn't comply. She wore no jewelry except for her diamond studs, which she unfastened and handed over. She'd miss them.

Meanwhile, the five other pirates had ascended the stairs and were entering the upper deck. Why wasn't anyone stopping them? The bosun was standing next to her, and she whispered, "Security?"

He shook his head.

What did that mean? That there was no security? Or that security wouldn't defend the passengers? What the hell was going on? Fear made her knees weak, and she stiffened her legs. She couldn't lose her composure now.

They waited on deck for at least fifteen minutes as the intense tropical sun beat down on them. Now she wished for that champagne she'd disdained earlier.

One of the pirates wore a backpack. That seemed out of place. What was so important about its contents?

The other pirates appeared on the stairs again. Her fear took a giant leap. What would happen now?

The first one to arrive said, "No Garnier."

Garnier? That was her host's last name.

The leader looked at the bosun. "Where George Garnier?"

The bosun shrugged.

The rifle whipped forward as he slammed the butt into the bosun's belly.

The bosun buckled and fell to his knees.

The leader asked again, "Where Garnier?"

"Where you'll never get him," the bosun gasped between breaths.

The pirate brought the rifle butt crashing down on the back of the bosun's head. He fell, senseless, to the deck. The pirate looked around at the guests, his eyes cold. "You sit. No trouble."

Sadie dropped instantly to the deck. The man had proved that he was no one to trifle with. One pirate stayed with their group as the others headed for the stairs leading below deck. The one with the backpack unslung it from his shoulders as they headed down the stairs.

Her face and neck felt hot, and the top of her head was burning up. Surely someone had gotten off a distress signal. Help should be coming soon, right?

The deck, hot from the sun's rays, only increased her discomfort. She closed her eyes. An image of Knox's face appeared before her, and she wished with all her might to have his strong arms around her. He would protect her. He would keep her safe.

Then she took that thought back. The last thing she wanted was to have the man she loved here in danger with her. For that was what she'd admitted to herself in the long weeks of silence between them. She loved Knox with every part of her being.

With one eye on the pirate, she scooted closer to the bosun. His head was bleeding. She had on a shirt over her halter top, so she quickly removed it and put pressure on his wound. The man groaned and stirred.

The pirate looked over and frowned, but didn't come toward them.

She whispered, "Lie still."

She held her blouse in place as silence reigned on deck.

Suddenly an explosion boomed from below and the whole yacht shook. The passengers near her cried out. Had there been a bomb in the backpack?

Shots rang out, and men yelled in a language that she didn't understand.

A moment later, one of the pirates appeared, dragging Garnier with him. Another followed, firing back below deck as he climbed the stairs. Someone belowdecks returned fire and shots pinged off the bulkhead.

She grimaced. So that's where security had been. Protecting their boss.

The lead pirate increased his pace toward the stern with Garnier stumbling along beside him. She suddenly realized that there were two fewer pirates returning from below deck. Security must have gotten them.

The first pirate passed her, and Garnier met her gaze, his eyes wide and panicked. But before the pirate could descend the stairs to his waiting boat, two uniformed security guards appeared from below deck and started firing. People around her screamed in fear and everyone fell to the deck.

Garnier, obviously well trained, dropped, his weight dragging the pirate down with him.

The pirate behind Garnier fired back, and Sadie leaned closer to the injured bosun as bullets flew through the air, seemingly in all directions.

Something massive slammed into her upper chest, and pain exploded in her brain. She flew back onto the deck. Sound faded. Time stopped. Only pain existed. Blackness descended.

Chapter Sixteen

Knox shook his head. "I'm going. Don't argue with me, Jessica. You're welcome to come too, but I'm going no matter what." He tossed clothing into his suitcase as he spoke.

"Do you even have a passport?"

"Yep. Remember when I booked that trip to Africa and then had to cancel when Dad got so sick a couple of years ago?"

"Oh, yeah. Right."

It had been forty-five minutes since Sadie's agent had called Jessica, who was listed as Sadie's emergency contact. Sadie was in a hospital in St. Lucia with a gunshot wound to the chest. Details were sketchy, but she was currently in surgery to remove the bullet. Knox had no idea how serious her condition was. He'd already booked the next flight out of Abilene through Dallas to St. Lucia, as well as a hotel near the hospital Sadie was staying in.

He'd also booked a hotel by the Abilene airport for the night since his flight left at six in the morning and he didn't want to risk missing it. The last-minute ticket had been expensive, but that hadn't mattered. He'd have paid anything to be with Sadie. He zipped his suitcase and set it on the floor. "Honestly, sis, there's no reason for both of us to go. You have school, and the ticket was outrageous. I'll tell Sadie that I told you to stay home."

Jessica wrung her hands. "I know you're right. Still, I feel guilty for staying here, even though I think she'd rather have you there than me."

He grimaced. "I hope so. But I *have* to be there. I can't bear the thought of her in that hospital, all shot up and alone." He took a last look around the room. Was he forgetting something? It didn't matter. He had to go.

"I'll call you when I know anything, sis." He gave her a quick hug and strode for the door.

OUTSIDE THE OKEU HOSPITAL in St. Lucia, Knox paid the taxi driver. At nearly six in the late October afternoon, the sun was beginning to set and the sky was full of brilliant golds and oranges. He couldn't enjoy the beauty, though. He'd had no word on Sadie's condition, and his anxiety was overwhelming him.

He headed for the front doors at a jog, his suitcase wheeling along behind him, and asked at the desk for Sadie. She'd been moved to a room, and he hurriedly followed the directions he was given. The door was open when he arrived, and he found her in a bed near the window. Her eyes were closed. He reached for her hand, wondering if she was merely asleep or if something worse was going on. An IV bag hung from a pole, the needle attached to the back of her hand.

Her eyes opened at his touch, then widened in surprise. "Knox! You came!" Her voice was happy but so damned weak.

He smiled. "Yes, honey, I'm here. How are you feeling? How much pain are you in?"

"It hurts, but I'm better now that you're here."

He smiled and leaned down for a gentle hug.

She clung to him and he held her for a long moment. When he drew back, he said, "I've been terrified of what I'd find when I arrived. I couldn't get any information about your status while I was traveling."

She frowned and tried to sit up, then gasped.

"Hold on!" He clasped her shoulders. "Let's use the bed for that." He found the controls and raised the head of the bed. The hospital had recently been renovated and modernized, a fact that was reflected in the quality of care they were able to offer. Sadie was in one of the few private rooms. When he had her situated, he asked, "What have the doctors said about your surgery?"

She leaned her head back and sighed. "The bullet entered my upper chest near my shoulder. They said that I was lucky that it wasn't a larger caliber, because it didn't do as much damage as it could have otherwise."

She sounded tired. He shouldn't wear her out with conversation. "Thank God you're okay." He grimaced. "I mean reasonably okay. I feared the worst." He looked toward the door, wondering how many nursing staff were on the floor. "Is it time for your pain meds? You said you were hurting."

She frowned. "I'm not sure."

That wasn't good. "I'll go find someone and check." At the nurses' station, he was able to determine that she wasn't due anything for pain for another hour. He returned to the room. "It'll be a little while longer before they can give you something."

She reached for his hand. "I'm so glad you're here. I desperately wanted you with me on deck when the pirates were shooting, but then I realized that I didn't want you in danger." She squeezed his fingers. "I knew you'd keep me safe."

"Oh, honey." He brought her hand to his lips. "I'd have given my life for you." She looked so pale and incredibly fragile. He might have easily lost her. What in the hell would he have done then?

He took out his phone and called the hotel, letting them know that he'd be checking in late. Brushing a strand of hair back from her cheek, he said, "You close your eyes and rest now. I'm not going anywhere."

After a long look, as if gauging the sincerity of his statement, she closed her eyes, a lingering sigh escaping her pale lips.

He drew a chair up to the bedside and took her hand in his, needing that connection after the seemingly endless time they'd been apart. Soon, her slow, even breaths told him that she was asleep. Exhausted from more than ten hours' travel, he let his eyes close. Despite Sadie's condition, his heart felt light—free of pain—for the first time in months.

SADIE WOKE AT THE SOUND of a chair scraping across the floor. She opened her eyes and smiled as Knox frowned at the noise he'd made.

"Sorry, I wanted to let you sleep." He sat down beside her and took her hand.

She smiled. In the middle of the night, in the darkened room and in pain, she'd wondered if she'd dreamed that he'd been there. She squeezed his fingers. "I'm so glad you're here, Knox. You're going to be sick of hearing that soon. I can't help myself. God, I've missed you so." She met his gaze, and his eyes told her the same story.

"Have you had breakfast yet?" He rubbed his thumb across her hand, and tingles ran up her arm. Despite her injury, he still affected her in amazing ways.

"No, you're here early, cowboy. By the way, where's your hat?" It was kind of strange to see Knox without his signature Stetson on.

"I didn't want to deal with it while I was traveling."

She squeezed him tighter. "I'm so sorry you were worried. It must have been terrible for you." She examined his face. He had dark circles under his eyes and appeared drawn. The time since they'd last been together had been hard on him. Her heart squeezed, and she bit her lip. What a mess this all was. "How's your hotel?"

He smiled. "I barely noticed. I got there late. I hated to leave you last night. Then this morning, I showered and scooted out of there. I couldn't wait to see how you were doing today."

A young man came through the door carrying a breakfast tray.

Sadie sighed, wondering how she was going to face eating.

The aide moved the bedside table across her lap and set the tray on it. "Enjoy." He smiled as he left the room.

Knox must have noticed her reluctance. "Let me help." He cut a bite of omelet and fed it to her.

She looked into his eyes and found gentle kindness shining through. A wave of certainty washed through her. She couldn't live without this amazing man in her life. Not anymore. Her modeling career, her life in New York—nothing was more important than Knox.

KNOX CONTINUED TO FEED Sadie, though it was obvious by the way she chewed and swallowed that the food didn't appeal to her. But she had to get her strength back. She looked so pitiful. What had happened to her since he'd last seen her? She was practically skin and bones. He gave her another bite. "You're doing good, honey. We're almost done."

She gave him a wan smile. "What am I? A baby?"

He grinned. "That's right. You're my baby, and don't you forget it."

She laughed softly and opened her mouth for the next bite.

Something that had kept him awake even though he'd been drop-dead tired last night came to mind again. How could he talk Sadie out of working at this dangerous job of hers? He couldn't stand the thought of her being in danger again. She was always dashing off to some exotic place. Who was to say that something like this wouldn't happen again? He had to convince her that going back to work was a terrible idea.

Sadie closed her eyes and shook her head. "No more, please. I'm going to pop, I'm so full."

He chuckled. "I doubt that, but it's fine. You ate almost all of it. I'm going to make sure you do that at every meal from now on until you pack on a few pounds."

She moaned.

He laughed. "I mean it. Don't take this wrong, beautiful, but you look terrible."

She opened one eye. "How can I not take that wrong?"

He grinned. "Okay, you're gorgeous but you're too damned skinny. I'm going to fatten you up, so get used to it."

A woman in white came in armed with a stethoscope and blood pressure cuff. Knox got up and stepped away from the bed. Letting go of Sadie's hand and that connection with her felt as though he'd just cut off his arm.

Sadie's eyes never left him as the woman took her temperature and other vitals. He smiled encouragingly at her. When the woman walked out, he sat down beside Sadie again. "Have you had your meds this morning?"

"Yes, I asked for them first thing. I had a lot of pain last night."

Dammit. He didn't like the sound of that. "We need to tell the doctor. He should up your dosage or change your script. You shouldn't be hurting that much." He stood, wanting to go to the nurses' station, then turned back to her. "When does your doctor make his rounds?"

She frowned and thought for a moment. "I'm not sure, but my nurse said that it's sometime in the morning."

He sat back down. "I'll be here, and we'll ask him together." He took a deep breath. It was time to bring up the subject that had been on his mind all morning. "Sadie..." He should have thought more about what he wanted to say.

"Yes?" She seemed stronger after that good breakfast.

"Sadie, I've been thinking..." He licked his lips, then decided to just get it out there. "I don't think you should go back to work. I don't mean like right now. I mean, not ever."

Her eyes widened. "What?"

"It's too dangerous!" His words came out in a rush. "You travel all over the world. Something like this could happen again, and I couldn't bear not to be with you." He clutched her hand. "Sadie, I can't lose you. Honey, I love you. I've loved you for so long."

She sobbed and reached for him, then gasped in pain.

"Dammit!" He stood and slipped his arms around her, hugging her gently to his chest.

After a moment, she said, "I love you too. I can't bear the thought of living without you. Not even for one more day."

His heart leapt and he kissed her temple. "I love you so much, honey. More than you'll ever know." When at last he released her, he sat back down and said, "Will you come back to the ranch to recuperate?"

She nodded. "That would be wonderful. And, about my job? I agree. I never want to go through something like this again."

SADIE LEANED AGAINST the weathered mesquite fence post, watching the horses graze peacefully in the pasture next to the barn. The walk from the house had been good for her. She needed to get her strength back.

The doctor had insisted that she stay in St. Lucia for two weeks to recover before he would release her to fly back to the States. Knox had never left her side. They'd returned to the ranch two days ago, where Maddie and Jeb had welcomed her with open arms.

While in St. Lucia, she'd contacted her agencies in New York and Europe and let them know that she was quitting her modeling career forever. She wasn't sure what her future looked like, but the overwhelming sense of freedom that had come with that decision had given her so much joy.

A handsome dark-brown horse just a few steps away from her stomped his front leg at flies and blew air loudly from his nostrils. His tail swished against his muscular butt. The sounds gentled her mind, reminding her how much she loved this wonderful ranch and how lucky she was to be there, even if only for a short time.

She touched her fingers to her healing wound. She'd come so close to dying, to never seeing Knox again. Closing her eyes, she imagined her life ending, an eternity of never being with the man she loved so dearly. Tears pooled behind her eyelids, and she pushed away from the fence. She couldn't bear to think of that.

As she turned toward the house, she spied Knox sitting in the porch swing, gliding slowly back and forth. He raised his hand and smiled. Her heart leapt, and she increased her pace.

Out of breath by the time she got to the porch, she mounted the steps and joined him on the swing.

He slipped his arm around her shoulders and kissed her temple. "How's my girl?"

She smiled and leaned against him. "Tired. I'm so glad that you suggested coming here for a while. I feel like all my cares are behind me."

He pulled her closer and pressed his lips to her forehead. "They are. You don't have to worry about a thing from now on."

He pushed the swing into motion again, and she closed her eyes, entering a cocoon of peace and contentment.

When the swing stopped and Knox rose from his seat, she realized that she'd lost track of time. He surprised her by kneeling in front of her and taking her hands in his.

His intense gaze met hers. "Sadie, I've told you that I love you, but I'm not sure if you understand just how much." He took a deep breath, his eyes filled with deep emotion. "I love you with every ounce of my being. I love you so strongly that I can't imagine living another day, another hour or minute, without you in my life. Sadie, will you make me the happiest man in the world and say that you'll marry me?" He drew a beautiful solitaire engagement ring from his shirt pocket and held it before her.

Her heart pounding with joy, she threw her good arm around his neck, "Yes, yes, of course I'll marry you. I love you with all my heart, Knox." She wiped tears of joy from her eyes. "I can't wait to be your wife."

He stood and helped her to her feet, wrapping his arms around her and hugging her tight. "Honey, will you live with me here on the ranch? I'll build us a beautiful home of our own."

She laughed and nestled her head against his chest. "I'd love that, sweetheart. I'll sell my flat in New York, and we can use that money to build the house."

"Huh?" He drew her away from him so he could meet her gaze. "That's not necessary, honey."

She stared straight at him. "It damned sure is. There's no need for us to start this marriage with a big mortgage hanging over us, is there?"

He smiled and shook his head. "One of the things I've always loved about you is that there's a lot more to you than just a pretty face. I guess I'd better get used to it, huh?"

She laughed. "That's right. This marriage will be a partnership." She held out her hand. "Agreed?"

He grinned and shook with her. "Agreed, beautiful."

Chapter Seventeen

Several months later, Knox hugged his dad before stepping up on the dais in the small church where he had attended services growing up.

"Take good care of my sweetheart." He grinned as his dad rolled his eyes. Organ music played in the background, and wedding guests talked quietly among themselves.

"You know I will, son. I'm proud to have the honor of escorting Sadie down the aisle."

Blake clapped Knox on the back. "Quit worrying, bud. Your girl is used to walking runways. She'll be a star."

Knox adjusted his cuffs nervously. "I know she will. It's me who'll make a fool of myself."

Jeb turned and walked toward the back of the church.

Knox's gaze followed him, knowing that he was going to find Sadie and that there were only moments before the ceremony would begin.

Blake, who stood beside him, bumped his shoulder. "Settle down now. Today's going to be perfect. I don't know what you're worried about, anyway. Rehearsal last night went fine. You know what you're doing."

Knox nodded. "I just feel sorry for Sadie, you know? None of her family is here. I want this to be the most wonderful day of her life."

"And it will be. Besides, she didn't want her parents here, right?"

Knox sighed. "Yeah, I know. It's just so damned sad, though. I can't imagine growing up the way she did." His hands, which were clasped before him, clenched. "As of today, she's got a big, happy family who loves her. She'll never feel alone again."

Suddenly, the organ stopped playing and the crowd grew quiet. Knox's heart began to pound. He stared at the open doors at the back of the church as the first notes of Debussy's *Clair de Lune* sounded. It was the music Sadie had chosen to have played as she walked down the aisle. Jessica, who made a beautiful bridesmaid in an elegant pale-blue gown, came through the doors. She was followed by their cousins' two young children, who were adorable at ages four and five as the ring bearer and flower girl.

He held his breath. Where was she? Then he gasped as Sadie appeared, more beautiful than he'd ever imagined. Her figure-hugging dress was covered in delicate lace. A sweetheart neckline tantalized his eyes, while lace sleeves highlighted her slim arms to perfection. A four-foot train trailed behind her, and she wore her veil back, exposing her radiant face to his eager gaze.

He smiled, his eyes glued to hers as she took one step after another, drawing closer to becoming his wife with every second that passed. His pulse sped, and he had to make himself breathe. This was his beloved. The woman he couldn't live without.

Jeb led Sadie up the steps, and Knox reached toward them.

The pastor said clearly, "Who gives this woman in marriage?"

Jeb said, "I do." Then he gently placed Sadie's hand in Knox's outstretched palm.

Knox drew her to him, barely resisting the urge to take her in his arms.

Sadie looked up at him, love brimming from her eyes.

"Knox and Sadie, stand before me," the pastor said.

Knox smiled at Sadie, guiding her over to the pastor and standing beside her. She clasped his hand firmly and leaned her shoulder against him. Jessica and Blake stood on each side of them as the children fidgeted nervously.

While the pastor spoke, Jessica took the little girl's hand. Blake did the same with the squirming little ring bearer.

Knox listened attentively as the pastor talked about marriage and the responsibilities that he and Sadie bore in their commitment to each other. This was important information. Knox wanted to be the best husband that he could possibly be.

At last, the pastor said, "Knox you may share your vows with Sadie now."

Knox had practiced so hard for this, but now anxiety gripped him like a vise. He said a silent prayer that his memory wouldn't let him down and turned to face Sadie. Her eyes were wide and full of love. His confidence returned, and his heart swelled with a rush of intense emotion, with so much love it nearly overwhelmed him.

He clasped her hands. "Sadie, my beloved, before I met you, I never knew what it was like to smile for no reason. I love the butterflies I get when I see your face. Honey, I know that I can meet every challenge life throws at me as long as I have you by my side. I can't imagine growing old with anyone else but you. Sweetheart, you deserve the best that life can offer, and I promise to spend every day of the rest of my life making you happy."

Blake handed him Sadie's ring, and he slipped it on her finger as tears flowed down her face. He wanted desperately to take her in his arms.

"Sadie, you may now express your vows to Knox," the pastor said.

Sadie gulped audibly and wiped her face, then clasped Knox's hand tightly. "Knox, you bring out the best in me. You make me strong, and you make me confident, and most of all, you make me incredibly happy. I promise to hold your hand, to stand right beside you, and to lend you my strength and support no matter what challenges we face. I'll be your partner, your lover, and your wife. I'll love you and encourage you, listen to you and advise you, and I'll be your best friend from this day and for the rest of my life." She slipped his ring on his finger and he clasped her hand.

The pastor smiled. "Sadie and Knox, I pronounce you man and wife. Knox, you may kiss your bride."

He swept her into his arms, lifting her from the floor. His kiss was enthusiastic and long as he swung her in a circle. The crowd applauded as the organ pealed out the chords of Mendelssohn's *Wedding March*. He set her down, and she clasped his arm as he escorted her down the steps. Their reception would be held right next door in the church hall and, though he was looking forward to celebrating this day with his friends and family, all he could think about was what would happen afterwards—his honeymoon.

KNOX GRABBED THEIR last suitcase at the Entebbe Airport baggage claim, excitement flowing through him in waves despite his exhaustion from the long, overseas flight. Coming to Rwanda to see mountain gorillas and chimpanzees in the wild was a dream come true for him. He'd always been fascinated by the endangered primates and, when Sadie had insisted that he choose the location of their honeymoon, it had been his first choice.

This was after she'd said in no uncertain terms that she was paying for their trip. He'd been totally against that, of course, but she'd put her foot down, saying that she'd saved most of her seven-figure salary every year and that there was nothing she'd rather spend it on than her honeymoon. When he'd still resisted, she'd gotten tears in her eyes and said that he was depriving her of a great pleasure by refusing her offer. Of course he'd given in. It was a major step in accepting that theirs was truly a partnership in every way.

"Ready?" He smiled at Sadie as he turned toward the exit. It had been an exhausting couple of days, but she was a highly experienced traveler and still looked incredibly fresh.

She nodded. "If all goes according to plan, our ride should be outside. Let's keep our fingers crossed."

Suitcases rolling behind them, they walked through the sliding doors to the crowded arrivals area outside the building. Moving to the side, Knox scanned the busy thoroughfare until he spotted a van with *Special Habitat Adventures* on the side. "This way, honey. The car's down here."

A man dressed in khakis waved at them as they began their approach. They'd submitted photos with their safari applications, so Knox assumed that this was how the driver recognized them.

Knox returned the wave and increased his pace, making sure that Sadie was keeping up. The crowd noise distracted him, and dodging through people who were standing still impeded their progress.

When they reached the van, the driver smiled and introduced himself. "My name is Sadiki. I'll take you to your hotel." He reached for Sadie's suitcase. "Please, get in. I'll load the bags."

Knox assisted Sadie up into the van and then slid in beside her, thankful for the air-conditioning as he shut the door behind him. Their safari group was limited to twelve people, and all of them would be staying at the same hotel. This evening, they'd have dinner together and meet the expedition leader. Right now, though, all he could think about was taking a good long nap. He squeezed Sadie's hand. "Sleepy?"

She sighed. "Boy, am I. I'm glad we got here in time to rest before dinner."

"My thought exactly."

The back door on the van slammed shut, and Sadiki climbed into the front seat. He glanced in the rearview mirror. "Is this your first time in Africa?"

"Yes," Knox answered.

"I've never visited Rwanda, but I've been to Africa before," Sadie answered.

Sadiki nodded. "Welcome to Entebbe. You'll find that the Rwandan people are friendly. Now you can relax. We'll arrive at the hotel in a few minutes."

Thirty minutes later, Knox tipped the hotel bellhop and heaved an exhausted sigh.

Sadie flopped back on the bed as she kicked her shoes off. "Lord, let me be able to fall asleep quickly."

He chuckled. "I know I'll be able to." He unbuttoned his shirt, then kicked off his boots. His socks followed.

Sadie grabbed a nightgown from her suitcase and headed for the bathroom.

By the time she returned, Knox was already feeling sleepy. He turned over and reached for her as she climbed onto the bed. The room was cool, but not chilly, so they didn't bother getting under the sheets. He gathered her against his chest, and she scooted her butt against him. He let out a long, happy sigh and kissed her hair. "Night night, beautiful."

"What time is dinner?"

"Don't worry. I'll wake you up in plenty of time to get ready."

She nestled her head a bit closer to him. "Love you, handsome."

He tightened his arms. "Love you, honey."

KNOX LAID HIS SILVERWARE across his plate and pushed it out of his way as he listened to John Stanford, their expedition leader, talk about their itinerary. He'd explained that they would leave tomorrow mid-morning for a flight to Uganda's highlands for two days of chimpanzee-watching in Kimbale National Park. Knox couldn't wait to see them in their natural environment. He reached for Sadie's hand and grinned. "Have you seen chimpanzees before?"

She leaned close and whispered, "No, and I'm looking forward to it."

Stanford went on to explain, "On days five and six, we'll be in Queen Elizabeth National Park. We'll take vehicles on safari where you'll have a chance to spot classic African wildlife like lion, leopard, buffalo, elephant and antelope. We'll also take a boat trip on the Kazinga Channel, where there's a large concentration of hippos. You'll probably see baboons, too, along with many of the hundreds of species of birds that abound."

Sadie leaned toward him again. "I really hope we see elephants. They're my favorite animal of all. I wish we could get close enough to really observe them." Her voice was excited, and he slipped his arm around her. What a wonderful honeymoon this would be for both of them.

He tuned back in as Stanford continued. "On day seven, we'll head to Bwindi Impenetrable National Park, where we'll stay in the Buhoma lodge for three nights. This is where we'll hike into the rain forest on days eight and nine to see the mountain gorillas. The mist-shrouded forest is home to over four hundred gorillas."

Knox took a deep breath as excitement coursed through him. His dream was suddenly real.

Sadie caught his gaze and grinned.

He gripped her hand and listened as Stanford spoke more on the subject. "We'll rise early each morning, and the trail up can be slick and steep. But it'll all be worth it when we discover the family groups of gorillas. There are three of them that are habituated to humans. No wildlife encounter can surpass the thrill of meeting these magnificent primates, which are so much like us, in their own habitat."

Dinner ended soon after, and Knox, his pulse still racing, escorted Sadie back to their room. He took her into his arms and smiled. "This isn't technically our honeymoon night since we spent last night on the plane together."

She grinned. "That so doesn't count."

"How about we order some champagne?"

She gave him a quick kiss. "Sounds wonderful. Dom Perignon 2010, if they have it, okay?" She yawned. "That shower earlier did me a world of good. I actually feel human again."

He went to the phone and called in the order, then gave her a slow smile. "Hope you're not still tired."

She grinned. "I think I can manage."

He laughed and covered the distance between them in two long strides. "Come here, you." He pulled her into his arms and gave her a long, deep kiss.

Her enthusiastic response set his heart pounding. He lifted her up, and she locked her legs on his waist. He chuckled. "That's more like it."

She wrapped her arms around his neck. "Kiss me again, cowboy, before room service gets here."

He brushed her lips with his, then delved deep, twining his tongue with hers. Damn, he wanted her so badly. He still couldn't believe that she was his wife. That she was his, forever and ever now.

She moaned and broke off the kiss. "Do you know how much I love you?" Her eyes were suddenly moist.

His heart melted. "I know how much I love you. More than I can express and too much for my heart to hold."

She cupped his face in her hands and kissed him tenderly. "I love you to the deepest depths of my soul. With everything that is me and all that I have and will ever be. You're my everything, Knox."

Her body pressed against the bulge in his zipper. He couldn't wait to get her naked so that he could show her just how much he loved her. He touched his forehead to hers. "We have the rest of our lives together, and I look forward to every single day."

She gave him a quick kiss. "Let me down. I need to change."

While she was in the bathroom, the champagne arrived. Knox signed for it, giving the young man a large tip. His grateful smile made the evening that much better.

When Sadie came out, he gave a low, appreciative whistle. She wore a short silk teddy in midnight blue. After spinning in a slow circle so that he could see her at every sexy angle, she walked over to where he stood by the table. "I'll pour while you get ready, cowboy."

"You don't have to tell me twice. Hot damn!" He grinned as he grabbed a pair of shorts and his kit from his suitcase.

He returned a few minutes later to find her holding two champagne flutes, her face plastered with a grin at the sight of him in his shorts.

"What? Can't cowboys wear shorts?"

She shook her head. "Those legs of yours ever see sunshine before?"

He laughed. "Hardly ever. Don't make fun of me, woman."

She handed him his champagne and took a sip of hers. "This is good. I'm glad that they had it in stock."

Grabbing the bottle, he took her hand. "Let's get this party started."

She laughed. "Lead on, handsome. I'm all yours."

"Damned straight, you are." He pulled her close as they reached the foot of the bed and grinned, kissing her before lifting her into his arms. "I have all night to prove that to you."

She chuckled. "I can't wait. I have a few things to show you, too, mister."

He groaned, "Do you know what you're doing to me?" He moved and yanked the covers down, then laid her in the middle of the bed. Climbing in next to her, he said, "Now that's more like it."

She reached for him and drew him over her, running her hands across his broad chest. "You're so strong, but you're so gentle too. You're everything I could ever want in my husband, honey."

He leaned down and kissed her softly. "I'll always be gentle with you."

She wrapped her calf around his. "I know you will." Then she smiled coyly. "Now, what was it that you were going to show me?"

He laughed. "How much I love you. Get ready, woman."

She grinned. "I'm ready, handsome."

He kneed her thighs apart and leaned his hips against hers. She pressed against him, eager for the contact, as she clasped his face in her hands and drew him down for a hot, sensual kiss that set him on fire. He rubbed his length against her, the feeling intensely erotic. She moaned and thrust her pelvis against him. He rolled over and yanked off his shorts and briefs.

Her eyes widened. "Me too."

He gripped the hips of her tiny thong panties and whipped them off. Then he drew up the hem of her teddy. "Now this," he said in a low, gravelly voice that he barely recognized as his own. She raised herself up, and he quickly slipped it over her head. He gazed at her full, rounded breasts. They weren't large, but they were perfect.

He took a taut nipple in his mouth, and she gasped in pleasure. Cupping her breast in his hand, he caressed her with his tongue, feeling her suck in a breath, knowing how much pleasure he was giving her. He moved to her other breast as she gasped, her delight mounting as his tongue worked its magic there too.

He slipped his hand down her flat belly and she quivered, then inhaled sharply as he moved it between her thighs and slid two fingers between her folds. She was slippery and wet, and he slipped them inside her. She gasped at the twin sensations of his tongue at her breast and his thrusting fingers at her core.

He loved pleasuring her. He wanted her to soar, to forget where she was, to lose touch with everything around her. He released her breast, and she whimpered.

He chuckled. "Hang on, baby. I've got you." She reached for him, clasping his face as he slid down in the bed. He'd taken a pillow with him; now he slipped it under her butt.

She ran her hands through his hair. "I love you, Knox." She spoke dreamily, lost in her response to him, and he smiled.

"Baby, I love you too."

The pillow raised her perfectly for his purposes. He moved her knees apart, and she sighed. She was exposed, ready for him to send her to the moon and stars, to make her leave this world behind in an ecstasy that would overwhelm her senses. He thrust his tongue inside her, then slid upwards, finding her sensitive spot, circling it as she moaned in response.

Her hands grasped at him as he did this again and again, caressing her, stroking her, thrusting deep inside. Her breaths came in quick pants, and she whimpered, her passion building. She pressed against him, and he took his time, loving giving her such pleasure. Suddenly, he knew that she was close. She spasmed and cried out his name.

"Come here, baby." He turned her over and lifted to her knees. "Is this okay, sweetheart?"

She reached behind her and grasped his hand. "Yes. I love you."

He was full and hard and didn't want to hurt her, so he entered her slowly. She pressed back, taking all of him. He withdrew and slid in again, faster this time.

She threw her head back. "Yes!"

He could feel her still pulsing as her orgasm continued. He thrust again, beginning his rhythm. She felt so incredible. He immediately worried that he'd lose it too fast, and he squeezed his eyes shut and concentrated. This was only the beginning. Tonight would be the best loving that Sadie had ever had. He had to make sure of that. He wanted her honeymoon to be perfect. Her breathing accelerated; her eyes were closed. Her face held a look of intense pleasure. He had to hang on. To prolong that.

Oh God. He threw his head back, his own enjoyment building in waves. She was made perfectly for him. Sadie whimpered again, and he couldn't help himself. Pleasure exploded inside him. His chest felt like it was going to burst. He pulsed inside her, ecstasy overwhelming his senses. Feeling his orgasm, Sadie pushed against him, wiggling, sending new waves of delight through him. He groaned and grasped her hips harder. "Sadie, baby, I love you," he gasped between breaths.

"I love you more," she said in a weak, trembling voice.

He laughed quietly and pulled her up to his chest, wrapping his arms around her waist. He kissed her cheek. "That was just for starters. A little quickie to get you in the mood."

A low moan escaped her lips. "Do I get to rest before the main course?"

He laughed. "I can allow that, I guess. But no falling asleep." He laid her down in the bed, then fluffed pillows behind her. He filled her glass of champagne and handed it to her. After filling his, he held it toward her. "A toast. To us and our extremely happy marriage."

She tapped her flute to his. "To us—and to a life I never thought I'd have and the man I've always dreamed of."

He smiled and took a sip from his glass. It was he whose dream had come true. He had the woman he'd always imagined. And tonight he'd make sure that all of Sadie's dreams came true too.

DAYS LATER, KNOX ENJOYED the view above him immensely. Sadie's sexy behind only added to the spectacular scenery. They were climbing a steep mountain trail in Bwindi's Impenetrable Forest. The guides had informed them early this morning that it would be a long uphill hike to find the gorillas. They'd also said that it was a good idea to keep as quiet as possible so that they would have an opportunity to see other birds and wildlife as they ascended.

The climbers had just gotten word that they were nearing the location of the most recent sighting of one gorilla family group, when Sadie's foot gave way. She cried out as she slid toward him. He reached out and grabbed at her butt as she came within reach, stopping her descent.

She glanced back at him, fear in her eyes. "Thanks, honey. This trail is so damned slippery."

"I've got you. Just be careful, okay?" He boosted her back up, watching her carefully to make sure she regained her footing. She had on sneakers, but Knox had bought a pair of hiking boots in preparation for the trip. He had a much better grip on the leaf-covered ground that made up the steep mountain trail.

A moment later, Sadie stopped and turned around, her finger to her lips for silence. He stopped, and as they'd been instructed earlier, turned to the person behind him and did the same.

A few seconds later, they continued on in strict silence, climbing in a more level area over vines and foliage until their guide signaled for them to stop. He motioned for the group to continue their silence, then proclaimed their intentions to the gorillas with amiable grunts, sounding amazingly like a gorilla himself.

Seconds later, he signaled for them to move forward, and suddenly they saw individual gorillas scattered through the rain forest. Mothers carried babies, and two youngsters played among the trees, seemingly oblivious to the hikers' presence. The mighty silverback, patriarch of the troop, held a stick in his teeth as he stared calmly at them.

A sense of wonder overwhelmed Knox. He stood frozen in place. He'd dreamed of this moment since he was a child and saw his first mountain gorilla in a National Geographic magazine. The silverback turned and gazed at him. Knox felt their eyes lock, and a shiver ran through him. The gorilla's intelligence was blazingly obvious as he searched Knox for his intentions with his family. Knox did everything in his power to emote love and caring and prayed that it carried across the forest floor.

Sadie was standing beside him, and he heard her sigh. One of the youngsters ran past the silverback, and the big male turned his gaze away at the distraction. Knox felt their connection break as if it had been a physical bond. He clasped Sadie's hand and grinned. She grinned back, keeping the silence. One mother held a tiny infant, and it started to nurse. She cradled it gently and nuzzled its cheek. Knox's heart melted. How like humans they were.

A pang of anger shot through his chest. How in the hell could poachers kill these magnificent animals? It broke his heart to think of it—it always had.

The guide motioned for them to squat down. Knox took out his camera and began snapping pictures. He didn't want to forget anything. He wanted to be able to relive each moment of this encounter for the rest of his life.

Several slightly older gorillas who looked to be teenagers came out of the forest and stared at them. Knox noted that they didn't seem to be nervous at finding a group of humans observing them. One climbed a tree and looked down on them, his eyes taking in each person in turn. What was he thinking? Did he think that humans were weird? Wouldn't it be wonderful to be able to hear his thoughts?

Sadie leaned against Knox, and he slipped his arm around her. She kissed his cheek, and he smiled. When he looked up, the silverback's gaze was on him again. The animal reached back and scratched his neck, his attention never wavering. Why did he find Knox so interesting?

Knox decided to make sure he didn't present a challenge to the huge animal, and moved his attention to one of the younger gorillas. He grinned as one youngster caught up to the other and sent him rolling across the forest floor.

Soon, their guide motioned for them to get to their feet and retreat. They'd been warned that their observation would be limited to a short time so that they wouldn't stress out the gorillas. Although he was disappointed, Knox understood that the gorillas' welfare was paramount.

Pausing a moment as the group of hikers gathered at the edge of the clearing, he took Sadie in his arms. "Thank you, sweetheart, for this amazing experience. It was the adventure of a lifetime." He stroked her cheek and kissed her gently. Life with Sadie, his true partner, would be an ongoing adventure, and he'd cherish every moment of it. With a last look at the silverback, he slipped his arm around her shoulders and they started down the trail.

Epilogue

Knox put the last dish in the dishwasher as Sadie dried her hands. They'd finished building their ranch house two years ago. Sadie had learned to cook all of Maddie's family recipes and was incredibly proud of herself. Some she'd made vegetarian, and Knox had grown accustomed to eating them that way. She'd blossomed into a country girl and, with Maddie's help and encouragement, had even planted a garden. Knox had tilled it for her first, of course. Now they had fresh produce for their meals, and he loved it.

A sound came from the back of the house, and Sadie sighed. "Damn."

He gave her a quick hug. "You grab a glass of juice and go on out on the porch. I'll be right out."

She sat in the comfortable padded wooden swing that Knox had bought her when they'd moved into their new house and looked out over the pasture where Sally contentedly ate the tall grass.

A moment later, the screen door banged behind Knox as he stepped out onto the porch.

Sadie smiled and patted the seat beside her. "I brought you a beer." She stopped the swing so that he could sit down.

He settled against the back, and gazed down at the tiny form he held wrapped in the little quilt Sadie had made. "What do you see with those big blue eyes of yours, huh? What do you see?"

Sadie grinned. "You always sound so cute when you talk baby talk."

He chuckled. "We're lucky she has your looks." His two-month-old daughter had been born the spitting image of her mother, and he couldn't be happier. His parents, over the moon at being grandparents, were happy to watch little Sage whenever Sadie had errands to run.

Sage's mouth began to work, and a squeak, and then a sharp cry, came from her.

He smiled at Sadie. "I think someone's hungry."

Sadie downed the last of her juice and set the glass on the porch. "Pass her over. This milk cow has plenty of dinner ready."

Knox laughed. Sadie, once a big-city girl, now had plenty of country in her. He'd been so happy when she'd decided to breastfeed their baby. He passed Sage over, and Sadie snuggled the baby to her. Their daughter latched on with a vengeance, and avid sucking sounds commenced immediately.

Knox grinned. "Nothing wrong with her appetite."

Sadie smiled. "She's a good eater. Like her daddy." Sadie caressed Sage's cheek.

He sighed and reached up to tuck a stray lock of hair behind his wife's ear. "I love you, honey."

She looked up, her eyes filled with a gentle devotion. "Sweetheart, I love you, forever and ever and ever."

He brought her fingers to his lips. At last, all of his dreams had come true.

KEEP READING FOR YOUR FREE BOOK

FREE BOOK

www.janalynknight.com

ALSO BY JANALYN KNIGHT

Cowboy for a Season
True Blue Texas Cowboy
The Govain Cowboys Series
The Cowboy's Fate
The Cowboy's Choice
The Cowboy's Wish
The Howelton Texas Series
Cowboy Refuge
Cowboy Promise
Cowboy Strong
The Tough Texan Series
Stone One Tough Texan
North Their Tough Texan
Clint Her Tough Texan
The Cowboy SEALs Series
The Cowboy SEAL's Secret Baby
The Cowboy SEAL's Daddy School
The Cowboy SEAL'S Second Chance
The Texas Knight Series
Her Guardian Angel Cowboy
Her Ride or Die Cowboy
Her Miracle Cowboy
The Lassoed Hearts Series

DEAR READER

Thank you so much for reading my books. Drop by jana-lynknight.com[1] and join my *Wranglers Readers Group* to be the first to get a look at my newest books and to enter my many giveaways. Or, if you like leaving reviews of the books you read, become a member of my POSSE Review Team at my Join my POSSE[2] page and get advance copies of my new books in exchange for leaving honest reviews.

You can also talk to me on Facebook[3] at https://www.facebook.com/janalynknight

Follow Me On BookBub[4] – You'll get a New Release Alert when my next book comes out.

Follow Me On Twitter[5] and be the first to find out when my books are on sale.

Follow Me On Instagram[6] where, among other things, you'll see some of the amazing horses from the refuge where I volunteer

Until next time, may all your dreams be of cowboys!

1. https://janalynknight.com/

2. https://janalynknight.com/join-my-posse/

3.   https://www.facebook.com/janalynknight

4.   https://www.bookbub.com/authors/janalyn-knight

5.   https://twitter.com/Janalyn_Knight

6.   https://www.instagram.com/janalynknight/

REVIEW

I f you enjoyed Knox's book, please leave a review. Reviews are the life's-blood of an author's living and are very much appreciated!

Review On Amazon

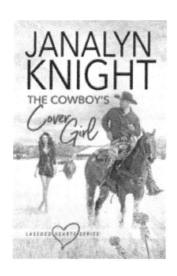

COPYRIGHT

The Cowboy's Cover Girl, copyright © 2021 by Janalyn Knight. This is a work of fiction. Names, places, businesses, characters and incidents are either the product of the author's imagination or are used in a fictitious manner. Any resemblance to actual persons living or dead, actual events or locales is purely coincidental.

About the Author

Nobody knows sexy Texas cowboys like Janalyn Knight. She grew up competing in rodeo, later working on a ten-thousand-acre cattle ranch, and these experiences lend an authenticity to her characters and stories. Janalyn is an avid supporter of the Hill Country Horse Refuge and absolutely owns the title of wine drinker extraordinaire. When she's not writing spicy cowboy romances, she's living her dream—sharing her twenty-acres of Texas Hill Country with her daughters and their families.

Read more at https://janalynknight.com/.